# THE *j*EALOUSY *b*ONE

# THE JEALOUSY BONE

STORIES

BY JULIE PAUL

EMDASH publishing
VICTORIA, BC

Published by EMDASH PUBLISHING
2341 Dowler Place, Victoria, BC V8T 4H5
ON THE WEB AT www.emdash.ca

Designed, printed and bound in Canada.

LIBRARY AND ARCHIVES CANADA CATALOGUING IN PUBLICATION
Paul, Julie, 1969-
    The jealousy bone / Julie Paul.

Short stories.

ISBN 978-0-9780182-4-5

    I. TITLE.
PS8631.A8498J43 2008        C813'.6      C2008-900008-0

*To Avery, my oval, my spiral,*
*my cinnamon stick.*

*And to Ryan, my Canadian Shield.*

# CONTENTS

RADIO WHO . . . . . . . . . . . . . . . . .3

STAKING THE DELPHINIUMS . . . . . . 17

BACKSTORY. . . . . . . . . . . . . . . . .36

LOVE AND MITTELSCHMERZ . . . . . .50

THE TRICK . . . . . . . . . . . . . . . . .65

FALSE SPRING . . . . . . . . . . . . . .82

APPROPRIATE. . . . . . . . . . . . . . 106

ANTIDOTE. . . . . . . . . . . . . . . . 117

THE JEALOUSY BONE . . . . . . . . . 126

INSTANT FAMILY . . . . . . . . . . . . 133

CHICORY. . . . . . . . . . . . . . . . . 149

FEEDING ON DEMAND. . . . . . . . . 163

FROZEN SHOULDER . . . . . . . . . . 171

BORING BABY . . . . . . . . . . . . . . 180

# RADIO WHO

**THIS IS HOW IT HAPPENED,** how it still happens, from time to time. Every time we meet a woman I know, on the street or at a party, she asks me: Did you fuck her?

I have to be honest, because she can spot a lie a mile away. Then I tell her it isn't my fault and she gets mad, because she'd rather have me proud and unapologetic. I have known a number of women in this town, and other towns, and I don't need to remind her that at 47, I am ten years older than her—I couldn't just sit around and wait.

She's not jealous, she insists. She just wants a complete list, and that's what I've given her.

Now, we're having a party, my wife and me, to celebrate our new house. It's not a *housewarming* because then we'd have to invite our families and that's not what we wanted. We wanted to have a good time.

It's the first time that we've gathered our friends together in years, and when we sat down and made our list a couple of weeks ago, I got a bit spooked by the names. Four of them in particular, women we both know, and know well. I knew them first, however, before my wife came on the scene, and now she is friends with all of them. I mean, *real* friends, the kind that would help you give birth or tell you their unabridged histories without blinking. In ten years she's made my past into her present. I have nothing to hide.

When the first one arrives, she tells me I look like shit. It's true. I forgot my goggles this morning but was too stubborn to buy more, so my eyes look like I've been studying and smoking up all night. It's a look she recognizes, and didn't seem to mind fifteen years ago, but I don't bring that up. Thanks, doll, I say, and give her a kiss on the cheek. Swimmers' eyes.

This woman, her name is Lorna, used to have spiky hair and long nails. Now, fifteen years later, she's got her hair down in a nice golden mane, like a waterfall of corn syrup. She's got two sons under ten who are wild and horsey—they have her teeth—and she's brought cookies, homemade ones with a label on their jar done up in calligraphy that my wife exclaims over and promptly displays on the buffet table. Lorna got divorced two years ago, when her husband had an affair with a preschool teacher.

So, I say, as the boys chase each other around the front yard. Life is good?

Mike, life is a living hell, Lorna says, smiling at me like a dental hygienist, as if I won't be able to reply.

What do you say to that anyway? I laugh. One of the boys starts to scream, and when he comes in, he's trying to hold blood in his palm but it's slipping out all over the new laminate flooring. Everyone panics, including me. Do you know what happens if that stuff gets wet?

My wife is an amazing person. An amazing *woman*. These ladies arriving at our house were basically girls when I knew them, not that I was robbing the cradle. They just had that spark of girlyness in them, like they were still actually growing. Sappy. I could impress them easily. You were a DJ, they asked? Wow. Trekking in Peru? Totally groovy. Into oral sex and blindfolds? No contest.

But my wife is not as easily bowled-over. I had to work at getting her into the sack—she wasn't biting at all, at first, not taking any kind of bait. She was all about the process, then, taking our time, getting to know one another in every way but the biblical. Finally I got the rationale: she'd been burned in a bad marriage to a British tennis pro. For God's sake. How did she ever expect a man in his position to keep a marriage together? I held my tongue and offered her my shoulder whenever she needed a hug, and from then on, I was Mr. Sensitive. Finally, that was my way in.

While the mothers have the bleeding boy in the bathroom, I mop up the splatter, then search for Carmen, my own offspring. As usual, she's in her room creating some kind of pastel masterpiece that will have the guests oohing and carrying on. You've got to frame that, they'll say, and I will simply point to the walls. No, they'll say. Not all hers. All I can do is nod and shrug. I am proud, it's true, but I can claim no credit. She gets all her artistic proclivities from mama.

Hi, honey, I say to Carmen, who's lying under the desk for this particular piece.

She gives me a quick hi without looking up.

Your friends will be here soon, I say, knowing she'll call me on it.

They're not my friends, she says. They're friends of the family.

Well, your best friend is coming, I say. That's one real friend. We're friends with Katie's parents, someone Carmen has played with since preschool, and I hope to God they get here soon. Can you come out now?

Dad, I'm in the middle of this.

Can you please not kick the wall like that?

Sorry.

Five minutes, okay? I say, then close her door. If I give her absolute privacy, I think the time seems longer. I have no idea how she morphed into a teenager while she's still only nine. It might have to do with the move, but we're making extreme efforts at keeping her in contact with the old crowd. It's not like we've moved off the continent. We're just a little more remote. Suburban bliss, I say to myself every time I drive along the quiet streets, passing perfect lawns and giant fir trees and nice motorcycles in triple wide driveways.

All right, so I sound like the middle-aged man that I nearly am. It's better than syringes in the playground. Our last neighbourhood is the one that everyone's been insisting will be the next trendy spot. They've been saying that for the past ten years. My wife and I were faced with installing security or moving. We chose this. We're happy.

I am in front of the hall mirror, checking my nose hair, something I've been having particular trouble with of late, when I hear Rachel arrive. She comes in without knocking and she's wearing even more bangles on her arms than before. They're like tree rings: when I knew her, she wore four, maybe five, but now, many years later (thirteen to be exact), she's got at least twenty on those limbs. She also has crazy hair that seems to require frequent pushing away from her eyes, so she's always jingling and clattering.

Heh-loh-hoh, she calls. Tinkle tinkle.

Yo yo, I say, coming around the corner. Whassup, girl?

Oh, Michael, please don't. You sound ridiculous. She grabs me by the shoulders and kisses both cheeks, nearly deafening me with the bracelets.

Where's Jeffy boy? I ask, hoping she's brought him so we can escape to the patio for a beer.

Listening to the end of the game. God, your driveway is huge.

Rachel and Jeff live a half hour's drive away, in the boonies, where she makes pottery bowls in her cosy studio and charges big bucks for them.

Yes, I say, not everyone likes to park on a lawn. Or get car sick every time they go home.

You're just jealous, she says, and she may be right. Rachel and I were the kind of couple who would pop into open houses just for the heck of it, like we were trying on the house for size. We had a lot of fun, making up stories for the realtors about why the house wouldn't work for us. Our seven dogs, our pool table collection, our open-concept worm composters, and so on. I always fell in love with the country houses, the kind where the kitchen was the biggest room and smelled like manure and banana bread, because it took me back to my grandparents' farm. Their old hound dog Frank, the big pot of applesauce on the stove.

Can I get you a beverage? I ask her.

God, yes. Vodka tonic. Twist of lime.

Rachel never says please, either, once she knows you. Because of her, I'm being extra vigilant with Carmen, making her say please and thank you to *us,* not only the checkout girls. But I know it won't last. Already, she's starting to show signs of surliness.

The third woman is named Sue, and she arrives a few minutes later. I met Sue while I was working one summer in the British Columbia interior, interning at a small town newspaper. Sue moved here a few years ago, looking to do more than report on the deer eating the tulips. (Although we do have our own nice little deer here, at this house; we wake up and there they are on the deck, steaming up our patio door with their breath.)

Sue and I run into each other now and then, at a coffee shop we both like and at newsworthy events, even though she is mostly a movie critic now and has a weekly column in the free paper. She's tall, Sue, and seems made of cardboard. I remember wanting to fold her, the way a priest will fold the big communion wafer into four before laying it on his tongue.

Now I look at the way she holds her neck and wonder if she had rods put in her spine as a child, but of course I know the answer, because I have felt that spine before. That may have been part of the fascination when we started seeing each other. More likely it was proximity and her sparkling interview skills. This woman could get a four-page conversation out of a baby.

She stands at the door and takes a surveying look. Let me guess, she says. A rec room in the basement, a fake marble vanity in the bathroom, an electric can opener mounted on the kitchen wall, a pile of uprooted shag in the back yard.

We had the carpet taken away before the party, I say. But damn, you're good.

She gives me a hug and it feels like hugging a coat rack. Dear, stiff Sue.

Come in, I say. The action's in the kitchen.

She follows me, and once I'm in there, the total count of men is up to three. But do you hear me complaining?

The thing about having any of these women at my house is this: I imagine them here permanently. If I close one eye, the one seeing my wife, in the other eye I see a different woman in my kitchen. How can I help it? We all imagine these "what if" scenarios. We all wish we could go back to at least one lover, check in on them and their waistline or hairline, give them a little squeeze. My history is parading through my hallways, assessing the bookshelves, looking for traces of itself, high-grading the appetizer plates. It may sound cheesy, but it's like being in a dream. Of course I would choose what I have now. It's just interesting to have these pseudo-flashbacks.

After I get the men settled into a poker game in the basement, I take Carmen aside. She's been sitting in the furthest corner of the couch, still as a waterless fountain. Katie and her flaky family have still not arrived.

What's wrong? I say, instead of what I want to say, which is, you're making me look really bad.

Nothing. She doesn't move a muscle.

Do you want to take the other kids up to the roof? We have a strange rooftop patio with a low wall around it, where I've recently set up a ping-pong table. I just bought a box of 100 balls, too, after a week of climbing onto the roof to collect them from the gutters.

No, she says. That's boring.

Well, what then? I know she'll say a movie, but her mother has said no DVDs until it's dark out, trying to prove something, I guess, as if she is still the organic, no plastic, granola girl I married.

Carmen shrugs.

How about setting up a game of Monopoly?

She shakes her head and keeps staring at the wall, at a painting she did when she was four.

Can you take that down, finally? she asks. The elephant's trunk is all out of proportion.

I laugh. Proportion, I say. We'll talk about it later.

Dad, I was a *baby* then.

Then it comes to me. I've got it, I say.

She looks at me like I'm the dumbest guy around.

We'll set up a scavenger hunt.

At this her eyes flicker a little, showing some sign of life in there. She loves this kind of thing. We created an elaborate hunt for her birthday last year and she is always begging me to do another.

All right, she says. But Katie better get here soon.

I clink my beer bottle to her glass of 7-up, in a toast to our brilliance.

It takes us less than five minutes to put a list together. Ball, string, plastic bag, orange rock, and so on. I run to the computer in my office, type it in, print it off, and declare our intentions in the kitchen, where the party has concentrated.

Okay, I announce. Teams of . . . I do a head count and divide by two. Teams of seven. A mix of kids and old folks, please. Everyone shuffles into vague groups, Lorna's boys outside are separated onto different teams at her insistence, and I call out the rules in my radio announcer voice, leftover from my broadcasting days.

First team back with everything wins the grand prize, I say. Second team wins the booby prize. The kids laugh at that one. I have no idea what these prizes will be, but I will come up with something while they're out.

No crossing the road, I say, no raiding the Smiths' backyard, it's okay to go to the park down the street but no further. Then everyone races off, even my daughter, hand in hand with Katie, whose family has just arrived. Party rescued. Party cooking.

Everyone is hunting now. I am alone in my house, this new house I barely know. I walk around, straightening things up. I hide a few books. I pull a few others to the front of the shelf. I take a leak into our blue toilet and part of me thinks, suburbia is all right with me. The useless space, closets as big as the rooms in our old house, the spotlight on the living room ceiling highlighting the gas fireplace with its fake logs. It's all about comfort. I'm okay with that.

The doorbell rings. I don't know how I did it, but I forgot about number four. It's Jane, a woman I dated another lifetime ago when I thought I might have a bit of the poet in me. She's still at it, on the faculty at the university now, publishing little beautiful books every few years and travelling to extreme corners of the planet to gather material. A reporter, like me, but writing in perfect rhythm.

Hello, darling, I say. She reaches her brown hand out for me to kiss, and I do, smelling her skin and the rose lotion she has always worn.

Jane smiles, which is a wonderful thing to watch. After a lovely moment of grinning at each other, she says, I hope you don't mind, but I've brought a friend.

No, mais oui, it's fine. For some reason I have always spoken French to Jane.

I take a look at this person, this friend. She is in a black poncho and hat and big glasses, looking just like an artist I dated long ago, during my year in Montreal on a language programme. I haven't been back there in years, but I think of going east every time I see poutine on the menu. As if I'd order it here.

When she takes her hat and glasses off I nearly drop my beer. It *is* that woman. Veronica. A woman I haven't seen in over twenty years, not since I did something I still regret, which is that I took her to a party and left with another woman. I was wasted, tripping, full of excuses, but it was still a shitty thing to do.

She is looking at me now, at my generous forehead. At my gut. At my house with its stucco ceiling shot with sparkles to look like stars. Her face quickly becomes expressionless. Guess Mademoiselle Jane didn't tell Veronica whose party they were going to. And why would she? The odds of her knowing me are like what, one in a million?

Veronica, meet the lord of the manor, Jane says. Mike, this is Veronica.

And Veronica reaches out to me, like Jane did, fingers down. Charmed, she says.

I kiss the back of her hand so she won't feel left out, but I know my own hand is shaking. Likewise.

My wife walks in at this moment, followed by her team. They've come back first, and they've found everything I asked them to.

We won! We won! they shout. And, What's the prize?

But I've forgotten about the prizes. All I can think is, I have lied to my wife. One more unaccounted for. The list has just grown because of the sin of omission. I look around, desperately searching for something to offer them.

Go wait on the patio, I say. I'll bring you the prize out there. They troop back outside, everyone except my lovely wife, with her ruddy autumn cheeks.

Looks like we missed out, Jane says. Mikey, what have you been up to this time?

A scavenger hunt, I tell her and Veronica. They don't look disappointed to have missed it.

To my wife, I say, You're back sooner than I expected.

I can see that, she says. Hello, Janey. She is the only person I know who gets away with calling her this. She gives Jane a hug.

Jane takes care of the introduction to Veronica while I wrack my brain for some kind of prize. Luckily, Veronica alludes to nothing.

Halloween candy? We haven't even bought any yet, for what will probably be a monstrously busy night here in Familyville.

Then, for the second time today, I get another burst of inspiration.

I need your help, ladies, I say to Jane and Veronica.

They look at each other like I'm asking them to sing at BC Place.

Honey, I say to my wife, would you mind going out and assembling your group?

Mike, she says, in the tone meaning, don't do something stupid.

Once she's gone, I tell Jane and Veronica, It's easy. All you have to do is go out on the back patio and tell the group a knock-knock joke.

What? Jane says. Mike, what are you doing? Tell us.

You'll see, I say. Say it loud enough so I can hear you on the roof.

The roof, Jane says.

Shhh. It's a secret, I say to them both. Trust me. I don't have time for the irony now: I have made a promise about a prize and I'm going to come through.

I sneak out the front door and climb the ladder leaning against the garage. Soon I am on the roof, then swinging my legs over the wall of the rooftop deck, walking very quietly so no one down below can hear.

Then Jane, the good sport, says to the group, Okay, everyone. I've got a good joke for you. There is a general murmur of consent.

Knock-knock.

Who's there? comes the chorus of kids and adults alike. I peek out, and see that the second group has returned, and are waiting for their prize, too.

Radio.

I don't know this one, but it's off to a good start.

Radio who? they ask.

Radio not, here I come.

It's perfect. As soon as Jane says the punch line, I release the ping-pong balls from their box, and cries of delight rise to greet me as the white balls rain down. I stand up to watch the kids scrambling to pick them up and throw them at one another. Some are collecting them in their shirts, like apples, or snowballs. All of them look happy.

I catch my wife's eye, and she smiles, to my great relief. She grew up with Captain Kangaroo, too. She knows the reference, whether or not anyone else does. I am pleased with myself, I'm smiling back, Carmen is laughing and I have a feeling that the party will be a success. Then I notice Veronica in her black poncho, looking up at me as well.

Good old Mike, she says, loud enough for only me to hear. Good old Mike and his balls.

I know it's just a saying. But she didn't need to say *old*.

Most of the guests have moved inside again, kids still carting ping pong balls; Sue has left, always a slave to a deadline. I scan the deck for Jeff, or one of the other men, but there is no one left but Lorna. She's standing near the clothesline launch, an empty glass in one hand and a wet, slightly bloody facecloth in the other. Below, on the grass, her sons are rolling around, each with one of my ancient boxing gloves on. Who the hell told them they could play with those? I wonder. At least they're only hurting themselves.

Quite the boys, I say. *Boy* boys.

When she looks at me, there are tears in her eyes. I don't know how to handle them, she says. What will I do when they're bigger than me?

Send them over, I say, and laugh, hoping she will never, ever do this. I smack my fist into my palm. Whip 'em back into shape for you.

That's what they need, she says. Someone like you.

I wonder. What happens if you get the kids that aren't a good match for you? Carmen may seem like a stranger occasionally now, but before, through all of her life, she has been more of a friend than I ever thought possible in a kid. We have *fun* together. She knows how to make me think, and laugh, and be grateful for all that I have. Why did poor Lorna get saddled with these barbarians?

I reach out and wipe her tears away with my thumb. Things will get better, I say. I was a wild kid, too.

A faint smile is breaking on her face, a real one, not the kind she gave me when she came in. When I see that, I remember what I saw in this woman. Some kind of light comes on, a kind of glow, and before I know it, I'm giving her a kiss on the cheek, smelling her shampoo, and she's wrapping me up into a hug.

You don't know how lucky you are, she says in my ear. Her breasts are snug against me.

She's wrong. I do know. Ah, well, I say. We all have our hard times.

I'm facing the bathroom window as we're hugging. The curtain moves, and there's Veronica, checking out the view. I raise my eyebrows, the closest I can come to a shrug. She shakes her head and disappears behind the curtain.

I pull myself away from Lorna. Let's go get a drink.

Inside, I make the rounds with a bottle of wine in each hand. All four of the remaining women, *my* women, choose red, which says something to me. Don't most women move to white after a certain age, once migraines and hormones start coming on? Strong wine, strong women. It's an interesting pattern.

Carmen has taken to her bedroom with Katie. I can hear sugary pop music and manic giggling from outside the door, upon which her little wooden doorplate, the one decorated with primary coloured letters, has been turned over. Now it says, in black marker, KEEP OUT.

I listen for a few seconds. There's another voice in there. It's Veronica's. I noticed her looking at the artwork when she first came in. She's probably plotting Carmen's education, insisting that she go east to study, find a private instructor, and then what will happen? She'll turn into a little Veronica, complete with her own little Jane. I mean, I'm not worried about that. But still. Shouldn't we have a bit of input?

I almost knock. But someone in the living room, Lorna, I think, is calling my name. Best to leave Veronica where she is.

On my way there, I notice that the men have disappeared again. Jeff is probably entertaining them downstairs. He's good for a story or two about a failed business venture: he's always trying something weird on the side because he has such a dull job as a programmer. We sometimes tease each other about the past. I owe him a turn with my wife, he figures. I tell him, if she's game, go for it. It's only fair, right?

Except I don't really mean it. She's not his type, I can tell you. And it might take more than a glass or two of red wine to convince her to jump in the sack with Jeff. I mean, the guy's okay—he's not Quasimodo—but I'm not sure she could look past the lack of chin.

Rachel confided in my wife once. He has a larger than normal cock, she told her. In turn, my wife got drunk enough one night to spill those beans to me just before she drifted into sleep. What are you saying? I asked her. Am I the baseline? She shook her head, smiling. Go to sleep, silly. Now I think about this every damn time I see Jeff. I feel like I'm in a sit-com. It's not like I want to see it or anything. But what has Rachel said to him about me?

And there he is, on the couch in front of the window, his head's reflection beaming back at me from the glass. He's beaming too, sitting there beside my wife, clinking glasses with her. His hand is beside—no, it's *on* her thigh. Rachel is nowhere nearby. And where has Jane gotten to? Suddenly our house seems gigantic, excessive. Too many places to hide away. And we're about to have a teenager in here?

They don't see me, not until I'm right in front of them.

More wine? I ask.

I'm good, my wife says, not looking at me.

But Jeff holds out his glass, all smiles. The other hand stays where it seems to be quite comfortable. I know that spot, you bastard. I like it too. White, please.

What does *that* say? I fill up his glass before sitting on the other sofa beside Lorna, whose sons are mercifully playing Nintendo downstairs.

Lorna, I say to her. What can I do to make your life better?

Mike, she says. Dear old Mike. She pats my leg. This time, when she touches me, I feel like all she wants is someone to sit beside so she isn't alone.

At least she's smiling. Just before Veronica walks in, I cover Lorna's hand with my own.

# STAKING THE DELPHINIUMS

**MADDIE GARDENS** to maintain her equilibrium. Every winter, she plots the design of her garden, and during the weeks Niahm is away doing his first tree planting of the season, eating lunch with plastic bags on his hands to keep the chemicals away from his sandwiches, she mulches and fertilizes and plants a hundred different flowers. By the time he returns for the May long weekend, she is thinning and watering her seedlings; then, until he comes home for good in August, she has her delicate, beautiful garden to love. It works better than chocolate, or yoga, or whatever other people do to balance out.

This summer is different. Niahm is not in a mosquito-infested clear-cut, sticking baby firs in the ground. Instead he spends most of his waking hours parked on the futon couch, reading and nursing his sprained ankle, an injury gained by riding a skateboard down a logging road in his bare feet. Every two weeks, he kisses his employment insurance cheque when he finds it in the mailbox, then goes back to his groove in the futon.

Today, while Maddie was getting ready to go to work at the dental office, Niahm started complaining about the flowers again. He's been ranting about obsession, complaining about the time she spends out in the garden instead of keeping him company, instead of making dinner. This morning he was after her for political reasons, since he heard, on the CBC, about people all over the continent donating bushels of garden vegetables for the hungry.

"Half the city is lining up for handouts," he told her. Unemployment is exposing him to way too much public radio: he knows the probability of precipitation in every corner of the province. "Why don't you think of them? They can't eat daisies."

"I have nasturtiums, and calendula," she said. "They're delicious in salad."

"Salad!" he said. "The homeless need more than salad. What they're asking for is roots." He flung his arms around like a parliamentary zealot.

Maddie stared at him. He had a soymilk moustache, something that was cute the first time he did it three years ago.

"It's what they said on the CBC," he said. "Carrots. Potatoes. Something to keep them going."

She put on her jacket. "I'm going to be late," she said, loading up her bike bag with a thermos of soup and two bananas. "Why don't you dig up that empty section where the cats poop? You can plant the old potatoes from under the sink."

"What? You think I want toxoplasmosis? That cat shit is lethal."

She turned to face him at the door. "Only if you're pregnant. Listen, I'll see you later. Would you mind taking the blue box out?"

"I'm in my boxers," he said. "Can't you do it?"

Outside, their neighbour Bryan had just brought his blue box to the curb. Bryan was still in his pyjama pants, his feet bare. She watched him lean over his bottles and cans, separating the wine bottles from the jars. She looked at the clock. "All right," she said. "You're off the hook."

Shay and Bryan moved in next door a few months ago, and the four of them have started a back and forth dinner arrangement, each couple hosting the other one Sunday night a month. Shay and Bryan got the ball rolling with a barbecue last month and managed to keep the chicken far enough from the veggie cutlets to keep Niahm happy. "I know the sauce had anchovies in it," he said. "It tasted like cod liver oil."

Bryan is a bartender who wears clothes from the fifties with a brush cut to match. To Maddie, he pulls it off without making it seem contrived. She imagines Bryan behind his bar, telling dirty jokes to married women and making them blush. He's the kind, she knows, who would hold you close with the lights low and dance without music, the kind who would whisper with a hot mouth, a body that would grab on tight and not let go until morning. The sort who would teach a girl to play pool, and darts, and hooky. Niahm thinks he tries too hard, that he's too eagerly hip. "I'll bet you he gets facials," he tells Maddie. "I'll bet you he gets his chest waxed."

Shay has a penchant for vintage velvet coats. She wears her hair like it's another face, a venue for various colours and jewelled barrettes. Her favourite drink is a double macchiato, but when Maddie mentions muesli, her favourite cereal, Shay has no idea what she's talking about. She works at an upscale French bistro in Chinatown and believes the stone lions of the Gates of Harmonious Interest keep her safe at night when she waits for the bus beside the junkies. Niahm tells her to take a self-defense course. She just laughs and tells him she knows karate, and nine other Chinese words.

On Canada Day, it was Maddie and Niahm's first turn to host. Over a Thai green curry, made without fish sauce, the discussion turned to the politics of fireworks. Niahm hated fireworks on principle, believing that there were better, cheaper ways to celebrate; but, true to his shifting-ideologies approach, he was now up in arms after hearing that Quebec was getting more than its fair share of the federal funding for pyrotechnics, and had used it for St. Jean-Baptiste Day instead of

Canada Day. "It's a sham," he proclaimed, rearranging his injured ankle on a stool. "We're letting that province run the country. Aside from Montreal, I say, let them separate."

"All I ever wanted to see was the burning schoolhouse," Shay said, leaning over to play with spilled candle wax, pressing her fingertips into the warm red pools on the wooden table. Her nail polish matched the wax. They didn't know what she was talking about, until she explained: no one else had grown up in a village of a thousand people. "It was a cardboard school, the size of a McDonald's cookie box," she said. "With a slow-burning firecracker inside."

"You small-town girls had all the fun," Maddie said.

"We should bike down to the harbour anyway," Bryan said. "Celebrate our country at its loudest."

"Not me," said Niahm. He pointed to his ankle.

"I better not," Shay said, pulling her hands away from the wax to rub her temples. "I've got a splitter coming on. Best to avoid explosives."

"You know that migraines are linked to wine." Niahm picked up one of the two empty bottles of Merlot and gave it a shake a few inches from Shay's face.

"And caffeine, and sugar, and blah blah blah," said Shay, looking bleary-eyed and bored. "Bryan reminds me all the time. If I stopped living, sure, my headaches would be fine."

Bryan rolled his eyes behind her back. He looked at Maddie and smiled. "Guess it's just you and me, girl. Unless you're going to back out on me now too?"

She looked over at Niahm, who had opened the Globe and Mail and was about to ask for help with the Cryptic Crossword.

"Are you kidding?" she said. "Let's ride."

Maddie and Bryan biked to the lawn of the Empress hotel and swapped histories before the fireworks started exploding off the barge in the harbour. The whole time Bryan was talking about his passion for photography, Maddie watched his neck; in particular, the place where she had accidentally kissed him on a day in early June, when she had come home to find Bryan and Niahm in the backyard drinking Corona. She had given a peck to Niahm, and was about to give a peck to Bryan, but Bryan started to stand up for a hug. Her lips met that soft place on his neck just beside the trachea. She could smell beer and shaving cream and sun on bare skin, and when she blushed, he noticed.

"What made you become a dental hygienist?" he asked, handing her his water bottle. "If it's not too personal."

"A wee voice in the night," Maddie said. "I was called to serve the Tooth Fairy."

Bryan laughed. "A noble calling."

"It was the family business. My father was a dentist. I worked with him for three years, before he retired." She took a swig from the water bottle. It was filled with gin and tonic. "Oh, my goodness," she said. "You're bad."

He took the bottle from her and drank a mouthful. "Think of it as anaesthetic," he said. "Antidote for the crowd." They looked around at the families, some of whom had been there for hours, staking their claim on the grass with blankets and lawn chairs. There were a couple of children fighting over a neon glow stick, their faces covered with blue ice cream. "I wouldn't want to stick my hands anywhere near those mouths," he said. "I don't know how you do it, day after day."

Maddie leaned back on her elbows. "I'm not going to be in dentistry forever."

"I said that ten years ago when I started bartending. And here I am."

"But following your dreams, still," she said.

"Of course," he said. "We're dead if we stop doing that." It sounded rehearsed, the way it came out so quickly, as if he'd been waiting to say that for awhile. But she didn't mind rehearsed. It was better than Niahm rambling on about the weather patterns, making up improbable theories as he went along.

They talked about themselves for awhile, and then, eventually, they brought up their partners, as if to be polite. But when Bryan asked about the ankle, Maddie told him the truth: she was sick of it. When Maddie asked about the headaches, Bryan shook his head. "There's a new disease every month," he told her. "She's always coming down with one thing or another, and half the time, I can't remember what illness I'm buying her flowers for."

Full darkness finally descended at ten o'clock. They watched and counted with the rest of the crowd, oohing and ahhing above the children's screams, passing the water bottle back and forth, and when it was over they sped past the standstill traffic and took the oceanfront route back home. A few blocks from their street, Bryan suggested they stop to hear the waves. They rode up onto the sidewalk and leaned their bikes against the cement barrier.

A few weeks ago she had found a stone on this beach, shaped like an apricot: testicular, ovular, hermaphroditic. She dropped it into her pocket along with two fuchsia roses she had stolen from the cemetery across the street, full-blown and already dropping their fragrant petals. Stealing wasn't so bad if what you took was already on its way down.

She had placed the rock in her pot of lavender, nesting it among the silver-green leaves like it was incubating. Later, in a fit of nostalgia, she pulled the petals from the roses to sprinkle them on the sheets, something she had done once when she and Niahm had travelled to California. After a week of camping, the beige hotel room had been Niahm's extravagant gesture, the rose petals hers. But this time, once the petals were in her hands, she didn't feel like showering the sheets with them. In fact, after fighting the voice of obligation inside her head, a voice increasingly prone to laryngitis, she asked Niahm to sleep on the couch again. She reminded him of his snoring, which was really more of a purr. One pillow over her head would have easily blocked it out. The rose petals had ended up in her pillowcase, the smell of sweet decay keeping her awake for hours.

THE JEALOUSY BONE

As they stood there, listening to the ocean sucking and pushing the rocks along the beach, Maddie could taste gin and plastic and the briny air. When she accidentally brushed her hand against Bryan's he took hold of it, and kept it wrapped in his own.

"It sounds like static," Bryan said. "Like interference."

She nodded, and tried to let the sound wash over her, but all she could focus on was Bryan's hand, the warmth of it, the weight of his solid palm.

He squeezed her hand. "We better get home soon or Niahm'll beat me up."

She wasn't thinking of Niahm. She didn't want to hear his name. But now that Bryan had brought him up, she could picture Niahm, the pacifist, hobbling up to them, scrawny arms whisking the air. She laughed. "I don't think you need to worry."

LAST FRIDAY, MADDIE WENT to Vancouver to visit her mother. Bryan offered to take her to the ferry terminal, on his way to work, and she accepted, although it was twenty kilometres out of the way and much too early for him to be at the restaurant.

They took the back way to Sidney, the old peninsular road that wound through the trees and hills. She chewed her xylitol gum and rested her bare feet on the dashboard. He commented on her white nail polish, the same polish she'd been wearing for months. It was lasting forever on her toenails; everything seemed to have stopped growing except the flowers. Their lushness was a reminder, every time she stepped out the door, of her decadence, as defined by Niahm, her impracticality, her excessive need for beauty.

"I love coming this way," she said. "They even have trilliums out here in the spring."

"Ontario's flower," he said. "I went to Ontario once. They were everywhere." He was looking at her instead of the road as he talked. "We trampled them down, just to break the law."

She laughed, somehow overriding her inner recoil. This was what it had come to. Attraction that strong. That defiant. A rebellion against Niahm, everything he stood for, but also against parts of herself. She had been thinking about Bryan constantly since the fireworks display. And as for Shay, well, Bryan hadn't brought her up, or the fights they'd been having recently, or the words that floated down from their open windows like ash from burning paper.

"If that's the only law you've broken, aside from cocktails in water bottles—"

He was smiling. "It isn't."

"Theft?" she asked. "Murder?"

"Speed," he said. He wiggled his hands on the steering wheel and the van swerved gently into the other lane, then back again. "There's never been a more awful driver than me."

Maddie laughed. "Everyone speeds."

"You don't understand. I'm a menace on the road."

"Why don't you stop, then?"

"Are you kidding? It's what I live for."

Both of them laughed. But what Maddie had meant was, looking over at his unbuttoned shirt and his stubble glinting blonde and his eyes that were on her more than on the road, why don't you stop the van, right here? And in a rare moment of bravery, this was what she said.

Once they were on the shoulder, with the smell of crushed grass and clover floating in through the window, she climbed around the floor-mounted gear shift and straddled his bare legs in the bucket seat.

Bryan put his hands on her waist. "I don't think we should be doing this."

She could feel his cock growing between them, and she tilted her pelvis a bit. "I don't believe you."

He laughed, and with his hand on the back of her head, he pulled her face up close to his. "But it wouldn't take me long to change my mind."

After a few minutes, the heat of his hands on her bare shoulders, Wrigley's spearmint on his breath, the pulse of their position quickening, Bryan pulled away. "Your ferry."

Maddie brought her lips to his ear. "There's one every hour. My mother can wait."

"Good," he said. "Because I don't think I can." He pointed with his head to the back of the van, and Maddie moved from his lap to the foam mattress. He stood between her knees. "Can I take this off?" he asked, already lifting her tank top.

She raised her arms, and he slipped it over her head. Then she hooked her fingers over the waist of his surfing shorts. "These," she said, "are just going to be in the way."

**THE SECRET TO HER GARDEN** is good compost. Maddie is very attentive to technique. Sometimes, when she's turning the compost, she imagines turning up something living, something more than an errant potato; the decomposing waste from her kitchen feels matted, thickened, like cells, or scar tissue, the heft of a body below a thin disguise of leaves. At the very least, she believes she will end up with an impaled rat on the end of her pitchfork. She's scared one out of the plastic bin a few times and seen the tunnels it left. But nothing has ever turned up, except the dank smell of fermentation and avocado pits that stick onto the tines of her giant fork like olives.

Two days ago, the day Maddie got back from Vancouver, Shay opened her sliding door and stood on her deck. With a huge straw hat on her head, she watched Maddie work from above.

"That's a fun job, I bet."

Maddie could barely see her eyes; only her glossy, pink, Strawberry Bubbalicious gum lips stood out below the brim. "Not so bad."

"Your flowers really are incredible," Shay said. "Especially those blue ones."

"Delphiniums," Maddie said. "I'll save some seeds for you."

"Don't bother," Shay said. "I've come close to killing my house-plants, and they're all silk."

Maddie laughed. "Gardening's not for everyone."

"Bryan thinks it's a genetic default in me. That everyone should remember how to grow things, for survival."

She laughed again. "Do flowers count?"

"God, yes. We could live on the view from up here."

She liked Shay. She was sweet and innocent and easy to love. It wasn't supposed to be like that. She was afraid to ask, but she couldn't help it. "Bryan's at work?"

"No," she said. "He's playing paintball with his brother."

"And you didn't want to go?" Maddie said with mock surprise.

"Well, I had an appointment with my toenails." She stuck her foot up to show off the red nails.

Maddie laughed. "You must be very disappointed."

"You have no idea."

**MADDIE IS HOME AGAIN,** after a day which included being bitten by a child and being yelled at by a mother whose daughter wanted the purple sparkly toothbrush and got the pink one instead. Her hands, freezing from the fast bike ride and the abnormally cool temperature, would usually end up under Niahm's shirt, rousing a yell, and his warmth would bring her fingers back to human temperature. But not today. Not after spending her lunch hour making a mental list of what he would have to do to turn things around. Niahm is face down on the couch, reading *Shampoo Planet*. Still wearing his boxer shorts.

"The wind's picking up," Maddie says, dropping her panniers beside the kitchen table. "I'll be outside, tying down my plants."

"Your mother called," Niahm says, without looking up. "She was hounding me about getting a job."

"Oh?"

He looks up at her with a grin. "I told her I was pounding the virtual pavement. She had no idea what I was talking about."

Maddie stares at him. "Are you talking about the Net at the library?"

"It's not even worth signing up," he says. "You're only allowed a half hour a day. No, I was just trying to get back in your mother's good books. Man, she is one easy chick to fool."

No one has ever called her mother a chick before. "I see. Well, it doesn't run in the family." She starts for the door.

Niahm smiles again, with the book tented over his chest. "Aren't you forgetting something?"

She stops. Her mother used those same words every morning, on both her father and her, coercing kisses out of them before they ran out the door. She will never forget the look her mother gave her that day she refused, rushing to catch up with her friends. Rejection that obvious was not Maddie's strong point; she'd capitulated the next day, went back to the morning dole. But this time, she's in no mood to get within lip's reach. She starts moving towards the door again.

"Your helmet," he says. "You're still wearing it."

"They're calling for hail," she says. "I'm playing it safe."

She gathers the stakes and a bag of old nylons from the shed, then steals a glance at Shay and Bryan's house. The lights in the top floor apartment are on. She bends down and starts tying up the poppies, but not before removing her helmet and shaking out her hair.

On her ride home from work, Maddie had noticed a garden no bigger than a bath mat at the edge of someone's cement walkway. A few petunias, a couple of marigolds, some lobelia and alyssum, all planted tightly together: two times 99 cents for annuals at the Safeway. There was so much involved in this little space, so much that it meant to someone, that it moved Maddie to tears. A child? A senior? She wanted to show Niahm. Onions could have been plugged into the soil around a tomato plant. Salad mix could've been sprinkled over the patch of earth. But here, a heart needed beauty. Here, a person planted for love.

The wind had propelled her faster than she wanted, away from the little garden on Redfern, down the street, around the corner and, soon enough, she was swooping under ornamental cherry trees whose shadows lay like repeated psychological tests on the pavement. Home to a man who used to double her on his bicycle, pull her up the down escalator, take her to open air concerts in the square. A man who used to bounce back. She realizes, Niahm isn't a Niahm at all. He's just another Todd or Steve, saddled with a name that carries a mystique much greater than he can maintain. Having a hacky sack collection does not indicate enlightenment. Niahm is too lean for her, too thin where she would like thick, too righteous, with his meat-free ribs apparent beneath freckled skin. When he hugs her now, it hurts. His tongue is too cool—it feels like a pickle in her mouth.

She chose him, three years ago, because he was a risk-taker. Now he limps when he knows she's watching. The Sprained Ankle. It's become capitalized, a new roommate in the house. She has dreams of evicting it, beautiful dreams of empty, quiet rooms with the sunlight settled on the floor in wide bars, the scent of lemon soap wafting through. Is it cruelty when she piles his dirty laundry under his side of the duvet and waits to see his reaction? Or is it tough love? Or, simply, a change of heart? She is afraid of this person she is becoming. Someone so easy to rely on that it's all she becomes loved for, the way a kid sees a mother. She wants to give Niahm a shake; make him jealous; make him see what he's got to lose. Bryan could help with this. Bryan and his forearms. Bryan and his muscular ass—

"Can you believe this guy?" Niahm asks. "Calling his girlfriend 'his tornado'?" Niahm has come out, wrapped in her bath robe. He's talking about the Douglas Coupland novel, a book she read years before, when it was fresh.

"Listen, Niahm. I've had a shitty day. I'm really not in the mood for book reviews." She talks to him in her head like she talks to her annoying patients: Just go away. Just go away.

"But did you like this piece of crap?"

She can't remember. She stares at him intently. "Yes, as a matter of fact, I loved it."

"You're kidding." He looks at her like he's noticing, for the first time, that she has three eyes.

Maddie ignores him and keeps on tying up her flowers. She's staked up all of the poppies and is moving onto the lilies and columbine.

"Brrr," he says, shivering. "I thought this was supposed to be summer, for God's sake."

"Go inside, then! Or put some freaking clothes on, for once."

"What's up your butt?" he asks. "Why are you so cranky?"

Maddie looks at Niahm and shakes her head. "I'm just tired of it."

"Of what? Your job?"

"No," she says. "Not my job. Of this." She opens her hands and starts to spread her arms, but it looks like she's showing him the garden. She drops one hand, and points vaguely with the other at Niahm's foot. "This situation. Your ankle, your lack of motivation—"

"Oh, here we go. Go ahead. Tell me to get a job, like everyone else. Tell me to stop complaining about a sore ankle, when the rest of the world—"

"When the rest of the world at least tries. You haven't done a thing to get better."

"What are you talking about? The doctor told me to rest it and elevate it. That's what I've been doing."

"Well, don't let me keep you on your feet," Maddie says. "You better get back to your therapy."

She kneels to tie up a lily and seconds later she hears Shay on her balcony, calling her name. She's afraid to look up.

"Howdy, neighbour," Niahm says, and turns to Maddie. "Mad."

Maddie snaps her head into action to look up at the balcony. "Hi," she calls, although it's been too long of a pause without acknowledging her.

Shay doesn't seem to have noticed. "Can you come up here for a second, Maddie?"

Shit, she thinks. No, I can't. "Okay," she says. "Be right there."

"I thought you were cold," Maddie says to Niahm who's still standing by the side garden.

Niahm laughs, bitterly. "Not as cold as you."

Shay is in a black velour bathrobe when she meets Maddie at the top of the stairs. Does no one get dressed around here?

"Thanks for coming over," Shay says. "I know you're busy."

"No, no," she says. "I was just tying up my flowers." Maddie looks around the apartment and is shocked to see the mess. There are clothes on the couch—including the shorts she helped Bryan out of, newspapers open on the floor, and on the coffee table, a bouquet of dead tulips has dropped all of its petals onto the floor.

"I want you to feel this." She grabs Maddie's hand and puts it inside her robe, on the left side of her chest, just above her breast. "Is that normal?"

Maddie can feel Shay's ribs beneath her fingers, and below that her heartbeat, going wild. "I'm not sure," she says. "Are you feeling okay?"

Shay removes Maddie's hand and brings it up to her throat. "What about this?"

Her pulse is racing. Shay moves Maddie's hand quickly away. "I've gotta sit down." She sinks into a kitchen chair. "I don't know why Bryan's not home yet."

"What can I do? Can I get you some water, a cool cloth?"

"It's anxiety," Shay says. "I think it's a panic attack. My mother used to get them all the time. I just needed to ask you to feel it, so I would know I wasn't making it up."

"It feels pretty real to me," Maddie says. Maybe Shay doesn't make these things up. She runs the tap, fills a silver tumbler with water, and sets it in front of Shay. "What brought them on? For your mother, I mean."

"She mostly got them when my father was away on work trips. I don't think she could handle being alone."

Maddie tries to keep her face neutral. "And you?"

"Oh, I'm just stressed about work. I'm getting laid off in the fall and my boss won't give me a reference letter until the first of September. We had a little discussion last night."

"Shitty," Maddie says. "Isn't there something you can take?"

Shay laughs sharply. "Besides a vacation? I don't think so. But if Bryan would hurry up and get here, I could ask him to rub my shoulders." She takes a sip of water. "Oh, I don't know. Maybe if I don't think about it, it'll go away. Sometimes that worked for Mom."

"Just like bogeymen," Maddie tells her. "You stop thinking about them, and they usually go away. Bogeymen only stick around when they can smell the fear."

Shay laughs again. "I knew you would make me feel better. You're always so sensible."

Maddie pretends she doesn't hear her, but the words hit her hard. She *is* turning into someone's mother. She is too sensible. But is sleeping with your neighbour's boyfriend sensible? Is being in their apartment sensible? "Those are beautiful tomatoes." She points to the green bowl on the counter, filled with ripe beefsteak tomatoes. "Can I fix you a sandwich?"

"Exactly," Shay says. "Exactly what I'm talking about."

After putting two slices of bread into the toaster, Maddie gets the mayonnaise and some lettuce from the fridge. She takes them, and a large tomato, to the counter.

"You're a doll," Shay says.

"It's nothing," Maddie says. She has to clear the coffee mugs away before she can lay the cutting board down.

"No," Shay insists. "I mean it. Bryan and I are lucky to have such great neighbours."

Maddie is beginning to sweat. Her own heart is racing. "Same with us."

She washes the lettuce and shakes it dry, then rinses the tomato. As she slices it into thick discs, she thinks she can hear Bryan's van approaching from two blocks away. "Do you like butter and mayo on your sandwiches?" she asks Shay. "Or a slice of cheese?"

"Whatever you want," she says. "Bryan would disagree, but I'm easy to please."

When the toast pops she spreads butter and mayonnaise on both slices, lays the tomato and lettuce leaves on top, and sprinkles them with salt and pepper before flipping one side onto the other. She places the sandwich on a pretty plate she finds in the dish rack, and cuts it in two. She can do this. She can act normally. She can pretend that she has never seen Bryan's abs or inner thighs. Or kissed them.

"Oh, that looks incredible," Shay says. "Suddenly, I'm starving." She takes a big bite.

Maddie hears his van pull into the driveway, purring like an electric tiger, then clicking off to leave only the sound of the wind. She wants to look out the window above the sink, to catch a pure glimpse of Bryan, alone, but she doesn't look. Shay has heard it too. "Finally," she says.

This morning, when they met at the curbside with their recycling, they were as friendly as neighbours, nothing more, but Maddie could see in his eyes that it was an act. Of course. Shay could have been standing at the sink, doing the breakfast dishes. She could have been making notes. He asked her about Vancouver. He said he liked her helmet.

The van door opens and closes.

"Hey, man," she hears Bryan call to Niahm. "She's got you doing her dirty work, eh?" Niahm's laughter follows. Dirty work?

Maddie goes to the window at the top of the stairs to see what Bryan is talking about. From there, she has a perfect view of her backyard.

Niahm has been tying up her flowers. It looks like he's even tied up the snapdragons and calendula, plants that could easily withstand a twister. With trepidation, she searches to see the delphiniums, her babies, luminescent in the dusk. Their stems are hollow. They break too easily. She broke one herself, when she was planting gladiola bulbs behind them. Why the hell didn't she start by tying them up first?

But, from this distance at least, it seems that Niahm has managed to attach them to the sticks without injury, tying them up gently with her old pantyhose. Pantyhose he used to run his fingers up, from ankle to waistband, before peeling them slowly away from her body with his thumbs.

She strains to hear what Niahm and Bryan are saying, and she catches something about a beer, but Shay starts talking. "God, this is good," she says. "It must be true, what they say about red foods being good for the heart. Mine feels better already."

"Shaybey, baby," Bryan calls up the stairwell after they hear the squeal of the door opening. "Papa's home. You better be wearing nothing but a smile."

Doesn't he know that she's up here? Or is it just another part of the act, an act he seems awfully good at? Maddie's stomach balls itself into a fist.

Shay's mouth is full. She rolls her eyes.

Niahm's nervous laughter floats up to the women. "As long as you don't mind company."

Maddie can see a blob of tomato seeds on Shay's chest, a smear of orangey-red against the creamy expanse of skin between the lapels of her robe. She could leave it, pretend she doesn't see it, make Shay seems like a slob. But who is she kidding? She can't help it. She signals to it, pointing to Shay's chest, then her own. Shay looks down and giggles, then wipes them off and licks her finger. "I'm a mess," she says. "A helpless little girl."

After she puts the mayo back in the fridge, she sits down beside Shay at the kitchen table.

Two sets of feet are clomping up the stairs. Niahm and Bryan are laughing about something. What do they have to laugh about? And aren't the stairs too hard on Niahm's stupid ankle?

Shit, Maddie thinks. I'm a terrible actress. Something's going to show.

The wind is pushing the lawn chairs across Shay's deck. Instead of protecting her garden Maddie is up here, pandering to the hypochondriac. But is she making things up? When she looks at Shay, she sees someone reasonable, with a real problem. She sees a woman she could be friends with, a sad tomato, like REM sings, a woman who feels better because of a sandwich. Except that they will never be friends.

"Looks like we're having a party," Shay says, brushing toast crumbs off her lap. "I hope Bryan bought some wine."

"I have a bottle of red at home," Maddie says. "Good for the heart, right?"

Shay laughs. "Good for many things. Except headaches."

Bryan and Niahm are at the top of the stairs. Both of them are holding bouquets of flowers. Bryan starts humming "Here Comes the Bride," and they walk in, one after the other, taking slow, processional steps. Shay is laughing. When Bryan looks at her, Maddie feels like she is made of a million petals, all coming free.

"These were already broken," Niahm says as he hands Maddie a bunch of pale blue delphiniums. "What are they called again?"

Before she thinks about it, Maddie says, "Larkspur." She isn't lying—it's the English name. But for some reason, she wants to keep this from him. She knows he would prefer the scientific, the binomial nomenclature, something he could break down into meaning. She doesn't tell him.

"Larkspur?" Bryan says. "I thought that was a bird."

"Isn't that just a lark?" Shay asks.

"Whatever they are, they remind me of you," Niahm says. "Must be your eyes. Can you eat them?"

"No!" Maddie says. "They're poisonous. They'll make your lips burn, and worse."

Bryan laughs. "Sounds like a dare to me." He comes over to Maddie and sticks his face in the bunch of flowers she's holding. "Well," he asks, "do you dare me?"

# BACKSTORY

**MY HUSBAND** has brought me a raffle ticket. "Here's something better than Tylenol," Robin says, letting the ticket drift down onto my belly. I'm in supta baddha konasana, the only yoga position I can do with my back the way it is, supine on my aqua mat, feet together, knees out to the side. The ticket is blue. It says "Win a Dream vacation!" I close my eyes. Painkillers work wonders for meditation: the focused detachment is already there.

**WHAT WOMAN** thinks her back contains, at its base, a bone on the brink of mutiny? Who knows that her body is going to let her down while doing something as mundane as bending for the laundry basket with her knees held straight? My piss smells like an old sachet of potpourri, someone's idea of a drawer freshener without the fresh. Ibuprofen 600 mg, 3 times a day. The Tylenol 3's are doing something different, making my bowels into sausages, a bellyful of bangers and mash. The pain still lives: a sequel to a bad horror flick and the masked man just won't die. I've resurrected my comfort shirt from the floor of my closet. It's an old man of a shirt, a long sleeved black cotton waffle long ago turned green-grey. It smells like my new urine. I haven't taken it off in days.

**THE WORST PART IS,** I can't sit down to work. The computer squats on the desk, mocking me. The icons sit perkily in two rows across the bottom of the monitor's screen. *Your activities are being monitored.* I imagine an eye, trained on my movements, a camera controlled by a psych hospital escapee. Or, less maliciously, one of the neighbours. The one across the street. The one named Jack.

We met at our building's penthouse party six months ago, back in the summer. With his silvering hair, narrow body and Irish accent, he ambled over on the rooftop patio and offered me a sausage roll.

"That's my little home over there," Jack said, pointing to the window across the street, one floor up from ours and directly across. He kept putting his tanned hand on my forearm, pressing his points. "All I need for myself." His eyes were the colour of the gel inside a hot & cold pack. "My lady friend's trying to decide if she has room for me in her life." He rolled his plastic blues. 'I'm a wee man,' I told her, 'I don't take up that much space.'"

I kept arching backwards to accommodate his lean.

"What should I do?"

I could smell the zinfandel on his breath. His black eyebrows were like marionettes.

"I thought I was too old for this," he said.

Robin was still downstairs in our apartment making the dip for the next party on our agenda. We were on our way to his firm's annual BBQ, a morale-boosting / bonding experience that would leave my face aching from artificial smiles and daiquiri mix. The children of the other lawyers would be running around, bumping into the food tables, giving Robin many opportunities to look at me with smug horror.

"The heart doesn't age," I told him. But Jack didn't hear me, or didn't acknowledge what I'd said. A comment like that, ignored.

"Are you from Sweden, love?" he asked me, his face an inch from mine. He was staring at my blonde hair as if it were a new invention. "Can I get you another glass?"

"No, thank you," I said. "My man's waiting for me." I could see Robin in the car, waving street-side, three stories down. Jack's hand was still on my forearm, pressing a ridge from the edge of the patio's railing into my flesh. He made all animation leave his face, and stared at me with that look of his.

"Another party," I explained.

"Your man," he said.

"Good luck," I said. I didn't know what else to say. The sun was nonchalantly setting over the treetops. Robin leaned on the horn.

"Hit on by an old Irishman again, eh?" Robin said, when I gave him the synopsis. I'd been to Ireland once, before meeting Robin. "Are you trying to make me jealous?"

**THE COMPUTER ICONS** grin like perfect teeth.

**CRUISES HAVE NEVER INTRIGUED ME.** Spending precious holiday time aboard a boat, captive with other sunburnt tourists, comparing bargains from the afternoon's port-of-call. Judging countries by their cocktails. Wearing bronze flip-flops, white bathing suits with beaded wraps, sparkled strappy gowns: all dressed up with nowhere to go. Robin used to share the same mindset. We honeymooned in Algonquin Park, and now we cycle the Gatineaus on Sundays, wearing co-ordinates from Patagonia and Eddie Bauer. Now, he's dropping a ticket into my lap: fourteen days on the Aegean Sea. Is it the firm that encouraged him to do this? Maybe he's getting desperate, now that we've entered week number two of my sacroiliac nightmare. Maybe he's reconsidering his refusal to have a baby, and this is his way to tell me, hey, what the hay, let's go on a vacation before we do it. I don't know. What makes a man buy a raffle ticket?

**A WEEK AGO, THE DAY BEFORE MY BACK WENT OUT,** Robin came home from the hair salon holding a bunch of stargazer lilies in front of his face.

"Is the haircut that bad?"

He lowered the bouquet. "I just wanted to, you know, say it with flowers."

Lilies smell like hotdogs to me, boiled wieners in a kitchenette. "I love them."

His ears were red. He wouldn't look me in the eye.

"What is it?" I asked. "The haircut?" I knew it wasn't.

It happened the last time, too. Shelley used the razor on his neck, and Robin got a boner under the navy cape. He came home and acted strange that day: he washed all the appliances, cooked a curry, asked me to go out for a drink on a Wednesday night. Then he told me, after a carafe at the Greek restaurant a block from home, what had happened. It wasn't the shaving, exclusively, he said, but the way she had let her breasts brush against the back of his head. I've seen this woman: red brush cut, long neck, woodpeckerish. I wasn't that worried. The flowers were a new strategy, though. I wanted the equation: how many fantasies equal a bouquet?

"It's not bad," I said. He flipped me his look, a washed-out beach look, a what-the-hell-does-she-mean-by-that kind of look. "A bit short on the sides, though."

His let his held breath out. "Yeah," he said, running his fingers through Shelley's creation. "She got a bit carried away."

**JACK WATCHED ME** from the edge of the penthouse's balcony. I could sense him watching me as soon as I reached the sidewalk. He saw me try to get into the car, and waiting while Robin leaned over to unlock it. He watched my left leg going into the car and he watched my right one flex and enter too. He saw my elegant pumps. He saw me being driven away at instant speed in a black BMW. He saw my hand, delicately waving from the open window, fingers fluttering as if they might have had cobwebs on them.

**HE DIDN'T SEE ANYTHING.** There was nothing to see.

**WE LIVE IN OTTAWA.** More specifically, a part of town called the Glebe. Even more to the point, the Glib. We own a condo in an old apartment block: brick and hardwood, big windowsills filled with plants. We eat Lebanese take-out and strawberries on Haagen-Dazs. We swelter in the summer and freeze in the never-ending winter. There are three weeks all year in which you can enjoy breathing.

(I want to bring a child into this?)

(I do.)

The place was more bearable when Sharon lived down the hall. We became friends right after Robin and I moved in. I used to take tea breaks at her kitchen table, get my Tarot cards read, read passages aloud from whatever Oprah book I was into at the time. Now there's a middle-aged realtor in there who painted her celery green walls back to beige.

The street is a cul-de-sac, with the Rideau Canal at its end. Robin skates to work in the winter, carrying his soft-sided briefcase in a backpack along with his boots. He is smug about it, self-congratulatory, sends photographs of himself skating as attachments in his e-mails. He hates that I'm a west coast girl who never learned. I don't understand it, Robin says. Every Canadian should know how to skate. Lacrosse is the national sport, I reply. And I know how to play. Although I don't. How useful is that, he murmurs. It can't get you to work. I don't bother reminding him that I work at home, doing on-line career consulting. He calls it "the blind leading the blind." Is that politically correct? I want to ask him. You could get sued for a statement like that.

**SHARON PRESSURED ME INTO BUYING THE SLINKY BLACK WRAPAROUND DRESS.** I can't wear it, she moaned. Buy it and I'll live through you. Six months along, Sharon felt like she'd be pregnant forever. I promised to loan it to her once the baby came. Easy access for the milk. Then she moved to Vancouver three months after Carly's birth, when her mailman of a husband got transferred to that climate of mould and moss. The dress became the item that was never worn but got tried on every time we went out. The last time I did that, Robin came out of the bathroom in a towel and fucked me with the back flipped up over my head. I held onto the bookshelf and the paperbacks inched their way towards my fingers. We were an hour late for his Christmas party: I left the dress on. That night we did it again, on the living room floor, boozy and inexact. "You see what we'd miss if we had kids," he said into my hair. We both smelled like smoke and Obsession from all those seasonal hugs.

Sharon tells me that the living room is the only place they do it anymore, since Carly sleeps starfished between them. I didn't tell Robin this. "Let me take this off," I said, and tugged at the bow alongside my left ribs. "No," he said, and grabbed my wrists. "I like you better this way."

**AFTER THE YOGIC ASPIRIN WEARS OFF,** I examine the ticket again. Two weeks cavorting in the Greek islands. A dream vacation for the lucky couple.

I've been told all my life that I'm one of the lucky ones. The blonde hair, the strong constitution, the brain between thin-lobed ears. A smart choice, Robin Lefabre. A sensible man, studying law when I met him, and now on his way to junior partner in a downtown firm. A smart choice to love him. Did I have other options?

I never imagined myself with a man like Robin. He presented himself to me during the first month I was in the city, like an award I wasn't aware I'd applied for. I didn't even know I qualified. The usual courtship of movies and dinners ensued, a slow progression to the bedroom, a decent interval between engagement and wedding. I never wore Liz Claiborne until Ottawa, never a heel higher than the ground. Never, ever, makeup on Sundays. But these are the kind of things he notices. These are the kind of things he loves.

We look good together, I'll admit it, strolling along Bank Street with coffees, buying raspberries in the Byward Market, throwing extravagantly coloured leaves into one another's faces every fall. The leaves light the city up like flares. Warning, they say. You are about to enter a treacherous season. Warm up your shovelling muscles by raking us into piles. But sensible Robin draws the line at jumping in. He tells me there are hidden objects in there, waiting to hurt me. The children on every street he walks down in autumn get a lecture from him. A few steps back, I collect leaves to press in the dictionary and make the spiral sign at my ear: loony. Never saw the guy before.

**WHEN SHARON PHONED THIS MORNING,** I heard the baby in the background, playing with her ability to make sounds. "She's in her high chair," Sharon said, "talking to her Cheerios." Carly is nine months old, already pulling herself up at the coffee table, banging her head on the corners when she slips. I've reverted to the same stage now, I tell Sharon, hoisting my body onto its feet by using the furniture, not sure what to do once I get there. I feel like a mermaid, dragging my tail around, not meant for this side of the ocean. Everything below waist height is a mess: I drop something and it remains where it lands. Everything above waist height is in a shambles too, because I have used my limited standing time on other things. Staring out the window at the snow. Throwing out the lilies. Peering into the fridge and cupboards, looking for my lost appetite. And, early this morning, inexplicably, washing the black dress and hanging it over the shower rod. From wherever I am in the apartment, I can hear the water dripping onto the tiles. Little one-syllable drops. Oh. Oh. Oh.

**JACK REMINDS ME OF MY TRIP TO IRELAND.** There, I felt exotic, and foreign, and curious. In other words, according to my own judgement, I was a traveller, not a tourist. I stayed at hostels; I stacked bricks of peat; I developed a taste for bacon-and-egg pie. One afternoon, I picked stones from a field with an old farmer. He asked me to the pub for a pint and I said yes. Travellers are willing to try almost anything.

In Ireland, history mingles with the moment as if the physicists are right: time is irrelevant. There are no signs to the standing stones, the ring forts, the ruined castles. You can picnic on corn chips and Pepsi in the beehive dwellings of Monks from the sixteenth century. You can drink stout while a bodhran entertains you by a peat fire, then get back in your SUV and ramble home. You can bring your brood to the pub for dinner and not worry about bylaws.

The drink with the farmer was simply a pint at the pub. But when I arrived ten minutes late, to find him at the bar, wearing his sports jacket, suede at the elbows, his greying hair combed back from his face, I nearly turned around and left, unnoticed. All that hope in his shoulders, the waiting, the raw edge of his newly shaven jaw. It was more than I had bargained for. Then he saw me, and motioned me over with his head. "Thought you'd gone back to Canada."

At the well on his land, we had shared a tin cup. He looked at me, hair to feet, and told me I should meet his sons. All the girls are gone to Dublin, he told me. There's no one for them to marry. I pictured the life we might have, that sea in the yard, the green fields stitched by stone fences, sheep and children following me through the mist. I felt my face go pink. He was looking at me again. His wife was gone to Galway, he told me. Shopping with the ladies. They'd think you were a sight, they would. My sons.

After our pints were empty I let him kiss me goodbye, on the cheek. I didn't ask about his family. I counted the ridges around his eyes when he smiled and told him I would see him the next morning in the field. Then, just like all the Irish girls, I caught the morning bus to Dublin.

**JACK IS DIFFERENT FROM THE FARMER IN COUNTY KERRY,** other than his age. More like a ferret, less settled in his skin. After that party, before this skeletal interruption, I have kept running into him in the neighbourhood, his child-size red backpack strung over his sinewy frame. He's helped me take the groceries out of the car, and a few times even carried the potatoes up the two flights of stairs. We talk about weather and plans and whatever I'm wearing: he's always handy with the compliments. Once I told him I'd been to Ireland, he became even friendlier, rattling off names of castles and mountains and islands "I'd be daft not to have seen."

When I told him I spent most of my time in the southwest coast, he shook his tinselly hair. "Come over sometime, love, and I'll show you what you missed."

Predictably, his gel-blue eyes flashing. Predictably, my face rushing with blood.

**THE NEIGHBOURS UPSTAIRS WAKE ME UP NEARLY EVERY NIGHT** with their post-food-service, post-shooter couplings. Now, with my back the way it is, I can only lie there with three pillows beneath my knees, and listen. "You're gonna make me come, you fucking bitch." "You like it hard?" "Do you?" "Yes! Yes!" Robin sleeps with a pillow over his head and he's out in two minutes. I feel our bed shake with every thrust, feel the vibrations in my inflamed hips.

I'm a bit of a moaner too, at least when we go away. I wear the garters he bought, the heels; kneel on the bed with his hands on my hips and let my voice hang loose in my throat. But home is different. It's an old building. I stuff a corner of the duvet into my mouth, swallow my cries along with the taste of fabric softener. He laughs at the noise from above, saying it's a new relationship, that the novelty will wear off.

Today Sharon asked me, Doesn't it turn you on? As above, so below? I wish I could have said yes. But if Robin ever asked, "Who's your daddy?" I can think of only one reaction: hysterics.

What I said to Sharon, with sudden, hot tears, is this. Robin will never be a daddy. He doesn't want to become a family. He can't imagine dinner at a buffet restaurant, or staying at Howard Johnson's because the kids stay free. I didn't do the research. Anyone who knows him says he's always thought this way, but somehow I missed this little point in between the first date and the wedding. I'm afraid that he won't relent, and I'm afraid that I won't be happy, and I'm afraid that this problem I'm having now may be the most dramatic shift my pelvis will see.

**ONE AFTERNOON A FEW WEEKS AGO, JUST BEFORE CHRISTMAS,** Jack helped me carry an old washstand up the stairs. I'd found it at a flea market, and it was going to be my winter project. When we got inside the apartment, I offered him a blueberry muffin.

"I made them this morning. Robin and I got the berries in the summer, on our trip to see his folks." I rattled on. "Highway 7 is lined with wild blueberry stands. I counted seventeen."

"You're a regular Betty Crocker," he said, winking. "I might get fat with a girl like you around."

"How's your girlfriend then?" The lilt creeping in after only a minute now.

"Now which one would that be?"

I laughed, blushing. "The one who, you know, didn't know if she had enough space—"

"Ah, her. She didn't."

"I'm sorry."

"You've got a good wee memory, neighbour." He lifted a muffin from the plate I was still holding, and held it to his face. "A gift to the senses, you are." His eyes on me, a fleck of purple on his lip.

A comment like that. Ignored?

**AFTER SHARON HUNG UP FROM OUR PHONE CALL,** I thought about syllables, those little components of words babies say over and over, du du du, bo bo, revving themselves up for the language bit by bit. The sounds first, learning the way the mouth is held, the intention in the breath. All of this unexplained, just occurring with the greatest of intensity until one day—BAM—a sentence, then another, then they're talking and there's no going back. Like learning to love. All those stutters, repetitions, until you get it right. Or is it more like washing your hair? Do it once and you've got it, repeat if necessary. Sometimes I wash twice, just because I can. I would give that up, for the thirty-second showers that mothers take.

**WHEN I GET MYSELF UP FROM THE YOGA MAT,** I put the ticket on the fridge with our magnet of two cooks kissing. I notice how much snow has fallen since breakfast, and how the sky looks like it has plenty more to offer. I check the clock: an hour more to myself. Robin has gone to play racquetball with an associate from the firm, his regular Saturday appointment. I never imagined those words being a part of my daily vocabulary. They stick in my throat like a tortilla chip. Associate. Racquetball. The pain in my hip and lower back has eased a degree or two from the stretching—progress, however minor, for the first time since it happened. I take baby steps to the bathroom to run a bath. There's a note on the back of the toilet.

"Guess your back must be feeling better," it says. An arrow, drawn in orange highlighter, points to the dripping dress, a smiley face and a giant, confident R below it. "Meet you at the bookshelf."

**THIS IS HOW IT WILL GO.** Jack will be out shovelling the walkway to his building tomorrow, the first day I venture outside.

"I thought you might've moved," he says, casually, his bare hands on the shovel turning the colour of ground beef. I've had the blinds pulled ever since my back went out. So he is keeping tabs! He catches my eye; I feel the heat from my face spread downwards.

"Been under the weather," I say. "And do you think I'd leave without saying goodbye?"

"Nothing serious, I hope?"

"Just a bad back." As soon as I say this, the ache intensifies above my pelvic crest. "You better watch yours, all this snow."

"Looks like we're in for another shiteload tonight." He's scraped down to the cement, piling the snow on either side of the narrow walkway. The path is a dark scar in the snow.

"Seems like it," I say. I look up at the grey-white sky, the sun muted down to the size of a moon. "But we're going to Greece soon, so I can't complain."

His eyebrows do their surprised ramblings. "Are ya now?"

"In a few weeks." I've got the ticket; it lies in my purse like a fire-cracker. The draw is not for another week. I hold my purse closer to my hip. "I'm off to buy what we need."

"Aahh. Sounds lovely. My old bod could use a trip like that."

I will book two tickets for a cruise, exact replicas of the ones that will be given to the person with the winning ticket. There are some things I'm willing to take chances on, and others that I'm not.

"It should be mandatory, given all of this." I stretch my arm out, palm up, sweep over the snow-filled yard.

Jack shakes his head, smiling sadly. "Some of us aren't so lucky."

"I'm not lucky, either," I say. "Unless having a Visa card counts."

Then I realize what I've just said, and blush yet again, worried that Jack will tell Robin I'm buying the tickets. But then I get taken into Jack's intensive gaze. I'm suddenly aware of how little it might take for everyone's luck to change. One little twist and every bone goes off kilter.

Eventually, because I am still an optimist, because I am not ready to manipulate more than a fake prize—not yet—I will leave through the untouched snow beside the sidewalk, scalloping it with my boots, like a trail of brackets behind me to hold my words. As I walk away, Jack will watch my bad back turn good, in a light that makes everything that isn't white seem bigger, everything coloured bringing painful relief.

I will feel Jack, watching me, his blue eyes staying on me until I round the corner. Children will be throwing snowballs. Their wet mittens and frozen cheeks will hurt to look at, but I'll look all the same. I've gotten good at pain management.

When I join the fight—what's another few minutes?—and make some of my own ammunition, I will hear Robin's voice in my head as I bend to scoop up snow: use your knees.

# LOVE AND MITTELSCHMERZ

**WE'VE BEEN INVITED** to Randy and Lucinda's house in the country for dinner tonight. I don't want to go. I want to play sick, stay home, watch decorating shows and eat biscotti on our new biscotti-coloured sofa. I want Tom to make an excuse for me. Love is supposed to mean never having to eat with strangers.

We should be staying home anyway, both of us. We're trying to get pregnant. There still might be a slim chance this month.

Anyway, I had strep throat all planned out until last night when, right after our heated debate in the freezer section at the Superstore about which ice cream goes better with chocolate cake, Tom and I ran into Lucinda. Plans for faking a serious illness went out the window.

"Randy's bought a ton of seafood," Lucinda said. "He's doing his part to speed up extinction."

I'm allergic to most seafood; I puff up like I've been stung from the inside. "What should we bring?" I asked.

Lucinda waved her hand as if swatting away a fly. "Just bring your appetites and your hiking boots," she said, looking down at my feet. "We'll take a walk."

"I'm psyched," Tom said. "But Sandra's got an allergy to shellfish. Are you sure we can't bring something?"

"Not a thing. We'll have tons of food." As Lucinda manoeuvred her gigantic cart into the cereal aisle, she sang out a cheery "See you tomorrow!" The baby seat was filled with two dozen eggs and a bunch of green bananas. "Oh," she called out, "bring Karma, too!"

Karma is Tom's golden lab, left over from his last relationship. The woman is in India, renouncing possessions and aiming her heart at nirvana. She will gain enlightenment; Tom has gained Karma, a houseful of red painted furniture, and me. According to Tom, I appeared like an angel the week after she left town. Tom is full of these gems. He's forever calling waitresses and cashiers "sweetie;" everyone he meets falls in love with him. It happens so easily—I fell for him too. Sometimes, now that I know him, his positive thinking can veer towards corn-o-rama, but after a day of property showings at which I must exude an extra-strength, wish-I-lived-here aura, it helps to keep me sane.

Randy and Lucinda are Tom's friends, people he met during his triathlon period a couple of years ago, just before I came on the scene. He hasn't raced since his knee surgery, but he's just started to train again. He kept drinking the whey powder smoothies the whole time he was off; he kept his subscriptions up for the magazines. This determination is what attracted me to him in the first place. That, and the way his calf muscles look like two fish under his skin when he rises up on his toes. He tells me that's what the soleus muscles are named for: little fish. He pushes my hair behind my ears so he can see my zygomatic arches. He touches my ass and whispers, oh, sweet piriformis. It can be a bit much. Sometimes I just want to hear ass.

"Did you see her staring at my shoes?" I asked Tom, once we were out of earshot.

"I didn't notice."

"I can't help it if I need to dress up for work." I picked out four cans of Colossal black olives and set them in the cart.

"Sandra, a hairdresser's arches can't last eight hours in two-inch heels. She's jealous." Tom put two cans back.

"We have to buy four to get the deal," I said. "You got eight bottles of sparkling water."

"Water's different," Tom said. "I think we can survive without olives."

I put the two cans back into the cart, beside a set of glasses. I'm tired of drinking from the tall blue Mexican glasses, other remnants of the ex. I want to wrap my hands around a glass free of imperfections, a glass that doesn't lean to one side. "I raked it in this week," I say. "I'll buy these fucking olives if I want."

**BUSINESS IS THRIVING**. Interest rates are rock bottom, prices are sky high, and I have gained a reputation for selling condos to young, child-free urbanites like me, who really want houses on the water to kayak from but who also want the hipness of downtown. They end up with neither, but they still put their money down for the tiny studios I call "gems." I have a strategy I learned from my brother who sells coffee machines in Mississauga: I touch my clients on the upper arm, a slight pressure, a web of familiarity spinning from my fingers, then I apply the simple Principles of *Feel, Felt, Found*. Yes, I used to *feel* the same way about condos, I say. Most of my clients have *felt* the same way. But they've *found* that ownership gives them such a sense of belonging, owning their own small piece of paradise. I live in one myself, I lie. I wouldn't trade it for anything. (They don't want to hear that I still rent a drafty old house with Tom, for the character.) With my first paycheque, I sent my dear brother a mini-laptop made of chocolate, with this iced onto the screen: *Feel, Felt, Found my new calling. Thanks.*

Since I turned the big 35 ten months ago, Flare magazine's "perfect time for a career-driven woman's first pregnancy"—not that I listen to that drivel—I have been diligently charting my temperature in the mornings. I think I've gotten it down to a science: the books say the two days before the egg drops are the optimal ones to schedule the nookie, as well as the day it happens. Sperm can live up to five days inside. It's the egg that doesn't last.

I don't like this pressure. I'm not even sure I want a child, for God's sake, but Tom has been going gaga over every baby we run into. Think of the pictures, he tells me. Baby on Karma's back. Baby curled up beside yellow furry monster. Baby's face getting licked by giant tongue. When I accused him of just wanting to make artwork a la Anne Geddes, he actually started crying, he was so hurt. Okay, I said, once I saw that it wasn't just a whim. Let's give it a go. I was hoping I would catch the wave of enthusiasm once my egg met his sperm, but that still hasn't happened. I'm getting antsy: I want it all over with by the time I'm 37, so I can get back on the path and start selling, and living in, waterfront houses. I'm tired of exclaiming about the wonders of balcony gardening.

**AT RANDY AND LUCINDA'S** at 4:30, we find a note on the door. *We're hiking the old railway line. Come and find us.*

"I'll wait here, thanks." I follow Karma into the backyard, walking in her trail through the long grass. Tom throws a stick and the dog ignores it, opting instead to chase noises in the bushes where the property backs onto a stream. The clouds flash past in a wind too cool for summer; a neighbour's chimes tinkle, high and tinny. I sit down on a deck chair after arranging my sweater over the dirty white plastic. Why people with money still buy plastic lawn furniture is one of life's greatest mysteries.

"They didn't even wait for us," I say, although I'm not disappointed.

"I had to finish that webpage," Tom says.

"I don't care about the hike. But what kind of hosts go ahead without their guests? Especially when it's almost dinner time."

"They're pretty focused on their fitness. Or maybe they thought we weren't showing. In fact, I probably even told them to go ahead, if we were running behind." He rummages around in the right jacket pocket, then searches the left. "I thought I had half a Powerbar in here."

"That thing was ancient. I threw it out months ago."

The chimes have become drowned out by Karma, who is barking at a squirrel that's up in a broadleaf maple. "Cut it out!" I yell.

"Sandra, relax. We're in the country."

The dog keeps barking and stands on her hind legs with her front paws up the trunk.

"This isn't the country," I tell him. "Although these bugs are certainly a rustic touch." It's just a subdivision in the woods: I can see the neighbours' TV from my chair. I swat a mosquito on my forearm. "Shit. It's already full of blood."

Tom laughs. "Why don't you just give these people a chance? You and Lucinda might really hit it off."

I walk over to the hose at the side of the house to rinse off my arm.

"Are you grumpy because you're hungry?" Tom asks. "Honestly, you should get your blood sugar checked out. Hal's wife nearly killed him until she was diagnosed with hypoglycaemia."

"Right," I say. "I've hit the wall. All I need is Gatorade."

"Hey, I'm just trying to help."

"Then why don't you start the car? We could leave before they get here, and no one would ever know."

"Come on," Tom says. "Randy's an amazing cook. You'll be happy we stayed."

**I'M NOT THE JEALOUS TYPE,** but two nights ago, I picked Tom up at our favourite coffee shop after work, where he'd been talking business with a new client. He was sitting across from a woman in a black skirt and leather jacket. They were laughing. "Non!" she cried, reaching out and touching his chest. "Mais non!" As I walked up to them, he was holding his hands out in front of him. "Comme ça," he said, moving his fingers like flapping wings. Once he saw me he dropped his arms. "Quoi?" the woman asked. "Quoi?" "Hello, mon amour," he called, and waved at me, laughing. The woman turned to me and flashed her fancy smile. When I got closer to them, he said, "This is Sandra. Sandra, Monique." Monique said my name in a silky way, rolling it out of her curvy pink lips. "*San-dra. Enchantée.*"

I had ovulated the night before, and so we'd had tired, perfunctory sex again. For the past few months, I've actually become conscious of it happening, a dull ache on top of a pulling sensation in my belly. At first it was satisfying, a sign that this plan of ours was doable, like an offer had been placed. Now, after months of awareness, each time we don't get the timing right it feels like I'm a failure. Do we know what we're doing here? I want to ask Tom. Is an affinity for furry pets enough to make you a good parent? With all my research, I even know the goddamned German name for painful ovulation: every month, I get hit with *Mittelschmerz*. It's too much pressure. Why can't we talk about getting another dog?

"Nice to meet you, too," I said, staring at the woman's icy blue pendant resting exactly where her collarbones stopped to form a hollow. "Listen, I'm parked in a three-minute zone." I motioned to the street. "All I could find."

While they wrapped up their little tete-a tete and said their good-byes in French, I didn't wait around to translate. I marched back to the car, high heels driving my rhythm into the cement, and waited with Karma for Tom to come find us. "Don't you want a playmate, girl?" I asked her. "Don't you want a little puppy to wrestle with?"

Karma barked as Tom swung the backseat door open to throw his laptop in. As always, Karma was on his side.

**AFTER NEARLY AN HOUR,** the mushrooms on the lawn are starting to look appetizing. Then I hear voices from the driveway.

"Just in time," I say. Tom scowls at me before turning his sweetest face towards Lucinda and Randy, who round the corner of the house in lycra-poly blend workout co-ordinates.

"I'd hug you but I stink," Randy booms, sticking his hand out at me. I fix my sales smile onto my face, shake his hand and pretend to find him funny.

"We're used to it," Lucinda says, and Tom and I laugh like robots. "How are you, big girl?" Karma has her paws on Lucinda's abdomen, and she rubs the dog's head as if she's washing hair.

"Karma, get down!" Tom yells.

"It's all right, Tom. We have an understanding. Don't we, girl?"

"Come here, honey," Randy says, patting his thighs. Karma bounds over to him and licks his face.

"Karma!" Lucinda says. "I thought you loved me best."

"No shame," Tom says. "She's all about the attention."

"Aren't we all?" Lucinda asks. "Half of my clients don't need haircuts at all. Come here." She opens her arms so Tom can have his turn.

I laugh and run my fingers through my hair, subtly fluffing from the roots. Everyone wants to touch my beautiful Tom. Once she's done hugging him, Lucinda reaches over and picks a leaf out of my crown. "Thanks," I say.

She points to the tree I was sitting under. "Cottonwood. We've got to cut it down. You should see how much junk that thing drops in the spring."

"We?" Randy says. "Are you going to do it?"

"I would if you let me."

Randy laughs. "Your scissors'd get pretty dull by the time that thing hit the ground."

Lucinda says, half-heartedly, "Haw haw."

Tom interrupts the variety show by handing Randy a bottle of our homemade wine. "It's still a little green," he says as we all follow Randy through Lucinda's hairdressing shop and into the kitchen, past a mound of grey hair on the floor beside the sink. "A tad fizzy around the edge of the glass."

Randy puts the bottle in the freezer, grinning. "Just a bit of air," he says. "After a glass or two, I won't know the difference. Come on, let me show you the new wheels."

He steers Tom down the hall and into the mudroom, where, from the kitchen, I catch a glimpse of at least five bikes suspended from hooks screwed into the ceiling. The television in the living room is pouring out footage of the Tour de France. Karma flops down beside the woodstove and goes straight to sleep.

"This is Randy's famous clam chowder," Lucinda says. She takes the lid off the pot on the stove. "Help yourself. We're just grazing for now, and later we're going to barbecue some marlin. Talk about yum."

Does short-term memory loss come with using perm solution? I want to ask. What part of a clam isn't a shellfish? "I'll wait for a bit," I say politely, letting my stomach do the growling. "What's new with you?"

The artwork on the cedar-panelled walls includes an old wooden shopping list with plastic pegs to stick beside items you need—*milk, butter, bacon, cheese,* and a watercolour painting of a girl holding a rabbit.

"Oh, the usual," Lucinda says. "Work is work. Still trying to get knocked up."

My gut rolls the way it does when I've lost a sale. "Pardon?" Did she just ask me what I think she did?

"Pregnant," she says, laughing. "We've been trying for so long, I thought it was public knowledge."

"Oh," I say, trying hard not to show my relief. "I didn't know. But I hear it can take—"

"So how's work?" Lucinda asks. "Made any sharp deals this week?"

"Three," I say. "As my Dad used to say, it's like shooting fish in a—"

"How much would you say this place is worth?" She's right in my face.

I pull away. "Are you selling?"

"No, no," she says, putting a finger against my lips. "But it's good to keep track of the investment, right?"

"Right. Well. Houses in this area are going for between three and five hundred thousand."

"Give me a ballpark," she whispers.

"Oh, I don't know." I look around. The place is simple enough, but the property's got development potential. "Three ninety-five?"

Lucinda yelps. "You're kidding!" she says. "That's insane."

"What's insane?" Randy asks as he and Tom come back into the kitchen.

"Sandra was just telling me how much she pays to get her hair cut."

Tom raises his eyebrows.

"Oh yeah?" Randy says. "How much?"

"Fifty dollars," Lucinda says.

Randy shakes his head and points at his scalp. "Ten bucks and girlie mags while you wait."

Tom laughs. "He won't let you cut it?" he asks Lucinda.

"What, and miss out on all the trash talk?"

"They don't even wash my hair," I add.

Lucinda tells me to shut up with her eyes. I've only known the woman for fifteen minutes and already she's shooting me looks. "Okay," she says. "Who wants to play Cranium?"

"The Tour is on," Randy says. "Pas de games pour moi."

**WE ARE STILL THERE** at eight o'clock, plugged into the couches while the cyclists flash along narrow French streets and the men make bets on who'll get the yellow jersey. It's raining outside, Karma is still asleep beside the fire, and no one has made a move to cook any swordfish. My stomach is roaring with hunger. In desperation, I go to the bathroom and make my cell phone ring, and while I'm coming back out I fake a call about an offer that needs to be presented before tomorrow. Thankfully Tom plays along, and after we fend off the protests from our stellar hosts (but what about the huge marinating fish! what about the board games!), we're on the road again. We stop at AJ's Diner on the way back into town and order deluxe burger platters as soon as we sit down.

"You're having beef?" Tom asks when I tell our waitress: lately I've been veering towards the lower end of the food chain.

"I'm going mammalian," I tell him. "All that promise of fish has made me bitter."

"The salmon burger is to die for," the waitress chirps.

Tom smiles up at the nametag on her breast pocket. "Thanks, Tammy. Make mine salmon, then."

"Anything to drink?"

"I'll have a Canadian," Tom says.

"You're driving," I tell him. "You know I don't like to drive in the rain."

"Go ahead, love," he says to Tammy. "It's all right."

Tammy bounces away, and before we can get into any sort of debate about blood alcohol levels, she's right back at his elbow. "Your beer, sir."

Tom holds up the bottle and looks at it with eyebrows raised. "Never looked better."

Tammy leaves to buzz around other tables. "You just never stop," I say. "Nothing in a bra is safe with you around."

Tom starts laughing.

"Sorry," I tell him. "That French-Canadian client of yours wasn't wearing one. But Tammy, she's got a lot to control."

He just gives a little hoot, and shakes his head. "It took you two days to bring that up. I didn't know you were so jealous."

"I'm not!" I nearly shout. "I'm just honing my powers of observation."

Thankfully, Tom's honing his as well, because he notices some saltines on the table across the aisle from ours. He hops up and grabs two packets, and tosses one over to me. Just in time, too, because Tammy is bringing over a family to that booth. She's making goo-goo faces into the infant car seat. I tear into the plastic and place one of the salty squares on my tongue, letting it soften slightly before mushing it up and swallowing the gluey ball.

"You know, it's not their fault, entirely," Tom says after he's stuffed both of his crackers into his mouth. "We should have taken something to eat, especially with your allergy." He doesn't have to say *and your mood swings.* I can see it floating in a bubble above his smart little head as he takes a swig of his beer.

"They promised some kind of feast, then didn't cook it!" I say, although he's right. "Maybe because Randy was getting completely looped on our bad wine. No wonder they're having a hard time making a baby." I watch his face as I give him this last bit of information, waiting for the surprise to appear.

Tom shakes his head, then leans forward. He whispers, "He's got low motility."

"He told you that?" Would Randy tell Tom that? Would Tom tell people that kind of information about us, if we had that problem? *Do* we have that problem?

"No. Lucinda did."

Lucinda? "How long have they been—you know, trying?" I draw lines on my water glass, pushing the condensation onto the table in big drops. The toddler of the family is turning around in the booth to stand up and stare at the older woman behind them, who, naturally, is smiling back.

"Look," he says. "Isn't that cute?" He looks at me and says, "Three years," then cycles through a deep, cleansing, nasal breath. "That's not us."

I place my wet fingertips on my forehead, which is suddenly hot. I can see Karma in the car, sitting in my seat, staring out the side window at the light rain, then swivelling her gaze back to the restaurant. I think, I think—oh, shit, I think Tom is right. That isn't us. I'm not up for this gotta-get-pregnant club. If it were a priority, after all, wouldn't it have happened already? Okay, maybe not. But wouldn't I be dreaming of babies, lusting after rattles and Velcro diapers? "She wants out, you know."

"What are you talking about? Karma?"

"Lucinda. She asked me how much their house was worth."

"So? Maybe they want to buy another place."

"She was whispering," I say. "They weren't even looking at each other all night. And after the way he flipped at her for interrupting. What's so big about the Tour de France, anyway? Where's the thrill? It's not like tennis. It takes weeks to get through it." I'm so hungry I can feel my stomach starting to digest itself, little acidic pains burning through my gut.

"It's gruelling," Tom says. "It's an endurance sport. I can't wait to get back in the circuit again."

And where would parenting fit in? I want to ask him. Which one of us would be behind the baby swing, pushing our infant away from us over and over again? Do any of us know what the hell we're doing, anyway? Randy and Lucinda are sliding into a desperation so immense they forget to cook dinner for their dinner party. What kind of parents would do that? I want to ask Tom. I want to ask him a hundred questions about this madness. But just as I'm about to start, our glorious food arrives.

With platters held at nipple level, our benevolent server beams at us, and I practically grab mine out of her hand. Tom makes the thank you noises while I start scarfing. Both of us are so hungry that we eat in silence, until halfway through my burger, when I bite my lip.

"Shit!" I say. "I always do that." The family across from ours turns their collective parental head our way, frowns all around.

Tom smiles at them, so apologetic. "Is it that bad?" he asks, quietly.

I shrug and put my head into my hands. I'm not sure how bad it is. I can smell onions and mustard on my skin, and taste blood on the edges of my tongue.

He runs his fingers down my forearms, until he is holding onto my elbows. "Honey?"

I raise my head to look at him. "We can't be sure about our chances, either."

The baby in the car seat is tired of being strapped into a plastic shell, and is now mewling its little lungs out. The mother drops her bread and unstraps the baby, then pulls her shirt up and plugs a nipple into its mouth. Then, from their direction, a special bulletin comes flashing across my mental screen. *You won't be having one of those.* Not because it isn't cute, or tender, the way the child reaches up to touch the mother's face while she's eating, not because I don't think I could handle the pain, or the responsibility, or the overwhelming work, but because of this: my instinct was to muffle the sound, not to soothe the baby with a little bit of milk.

Tom's hands are warm on the inside of my arms, as if his blood could jump into mine straight through the skin. His thumbs are pulsing against my biceps, right where a child's head would rest while being rocked to sleep. I know the technique: touch the person, win them over. He's about to say something positive. Tonight, I'm not going to buy it.

"Only one in ten pregnancies ever makes it to birth," I tell him. "The odds are slim no matter how you do the math."

"That can't be right," Tom says, frowning. "Where did you get that? And even if it's true, it doesn't apply to us. We're the perfect age. We've got this thing aced. It's just taking a bit longer than we imagined."

I *feel* completely different than you, I want to tell him. I've never *felt* that kind of longing to reproduce. If you *found* another woman to carry your seedlings, I would have to let you go. I tell my clients this kind of thing all the time when their offers don't get accepted. Your dream home may be someone else's dream home, too, and it doesn't mean you won't find another one, even better than the first. "Flare magazine," I say. "It's true."

Tom presses both of my upper arms with his thumbs. "Don't listen to that crap," he says. "It has nothing to do with us."

I shrug. Then I wonder: did Lucinda ask him for a donation? That hug seemed a little too long to me. Didn't I see her actually rub his back a little?

"You know we'll get through this, right? We love each other. We'll make it happen."

Can love actually do that, instead of just getting me out of bad dinner parties? Should love alone make me feel better, turn me into a baby-producing machine, keep my hormones cycling through my body at a steady buzz? Is love going to feed, bathe, change, rock the baby, when I am not able to give any more? Tom would answer yes to all of these. Even if she begged him, I bet he would say no to Lucinda, because of a weird, old-fashioned notion that love needs to be a part of the recipe.

"What's the word for these muscles?" I ask, pointing at my bitten lip.

Tom uses his to smile at me. "The lips aren't really muscles. But the ones around them are called the orbicularis oris."

"It sounds like a constellation," I say. "Am I still bleeding?" I pull my lip out for him to check it.

"No," he tells me, then leans across the table to kiss it better. "But we should finish our dinners before Tammy takes them away."

He's a good man; he's so very, very good. My heart wants to give him everything he wants. Regular massages, breakfast smoothies, "adventure" weekends to celebrate anniversaries, dinner parties with plenty of food for everyone. Everything. Everything except what he wants the most.

"I'm finished," I say, wrapping the rest of my burger in my napkin for Karma. "She can clear up to her little heart's content."

# THE TRICK

*I will not keep this form upon my head,*
*When there is such disorder in my wit.*

William Shakespeare
*The Life and Death of King John*

**THE FIRST ISLAND** we come to is Small Skellig, rising up from the crayon-blue water of the Irish Sea like a giant whitecap. It's white with bird shit, thick layers of guano from the gannets and puffins and other sea birds that roost there, and they're shrieking and wailing as they circle, looking for places to land, warning us to keep away.

The guidebook is right: here are the roosts that the 27,000 pairs of nesting gannets have created out of anything they could find. Pieces of seaweed, rope, nets, even what appears to be a woman's sequined belt.

I want to stop and explore, but the boat forges ahead through the choppy ocean towards the bigger island, Skellig Michael. "It's just a pile of shite," says Finbar, the teenage boy in charge of driving the boat, when I ask. "And we're not allowed to land."

"Any puffins?" my husband, Jim, asks me.

"Not yet."

"Puffins?" Finbar says. "You'll not be seeing any puffins now."

"What's wrong?" I ask. "What's happened to them all?"

Finbar laughs. "They've flown the coop. Gone for a trip, they have, out from the coast to where it's cooler."

"But in the guidebook, it says—"

"That book's a piece of crap," he says. "The puffs won't be back 'til the spring."

I can feel Jim watching me. He's watching me try to swallow my disappointment, but I can't: like a multivitamin, it's getting stuck in my throat.

"It's all right," Jim tells me. "We're going to see an amazing sight here." He points at Skellig Michael, where Finbar is about to dock the boat. Jim is an architect, and the centuries-old buildings atop the island are more thrilling to him than any bird. Sixth century monks built a refuge from religious persecution on the mainland, and their colony of rocky nests has somehow stayed intact all these years.

I see the stone stairs that the otherwise useless guidebook has cautioned about, fringing the steep hillside of the island. I see the round stone dwellings at the top. I see no puffins.

I'm foolishly searching their habitat at the wrong time of year, but I can't stop my eyes from following every winged creature. A headache is creeping up the back of my neck from staring at the sky. I try and massage it out; it doesn't work. As Jim is helping Finbar with the ropes, I reach up alongside one of my ears and pull a hair from my scalp.

**FRIENDS HAVE ASSURED ME** that a postponed honeymoon can still be romantic—even ten years after a marriage. As good as the real thing, they say. Maybe better. And so here we are, in Ireland, day-tripping off the Kerry coast with five other tourists onboard with us. We are all at the mercy of Finbar, and the sea, as it rolls beneath us. We smile bravely at one another, Jim and me, but instead of thinking about love and passion all I want is to find a bird. A puffin. It has to be a puffin.

My father told me about them when I was a kid, in a tone he reserved for goblins and baby Jesus. He sailed around Ireland as a young man, stopping in a few places to work and build a fondness for whisky. They're a phantasmagorical mix of penguin and parrot, he raved. You can't believe it until you see one.

I recently looked it up—*phantasmagorical* is actually a word. I haven't been able to rid my mind of these birds, and now, more than ever, it seems important that I see one.

At home in Toronto, my father is dying. The man in the long-term care bed can barely see at all: diabetes has eaten holes in his blood vessels and his organs are failing one by one. I'm not supposed to know this. Eight years ago, Jim and I wrote him off as a hopeless drunk and cut him out of our lives. One too many times, he went over the line.

Now I am doing something Jim doesn't know about. For months, I have been secretly visiting my father once a week.

**NEITHER OF US MENTIONS** my condition at home. We know it by name, but we don't name it, except in our heads. *Trichotillomania*. It has an internal rhythm, a sing-song quality with its seven syllables and three stresses, and occasionally it comes into my mind, like a chant, when we're taking our after-dinner walk.

We called it "the trick" at first, when we used to talk about it, just after our wedding. Jim couldn't help but notice my hands digging in the hair around the base of my skull every few minutes, and he asked me what I was looking for.

"Nothing," I told him. "I'm just stressed." I showed him the list of life stressors, how marriage was in the top ten.

"It's weird," he said. "You look sort of, well, infected."

Finally, after repeatedly assuring him that I didn't have head lice, or scabies, or anything contagious, I admitted to pulling my hair out.

I've done it since I was twelve, after I was parcelled off to my aunt's farm for the summer while my parents sold the house and moved into separate apartments. When summer was over, I went to live with my mother. I had thick blonde hair. No one noticed anything for months.

"A lot of people do it," I said. "It's even in Shakespeare."

"Where?" he asked. "In what plays?"

I couldn't remember. I tried to downplay the whole thing. At least I didn't touch my eyebrows or lashes, or eat the root bulb the way others did, although I did touch it, to feel its richness, its area of contact with the inside of my body. Some people with the condition have no facial hair left at all. The doctor I had seen when I was fourteen, after Mom caught on, seemed to think I was going to recover in a matter of months. He had recommended a cat, as therapy, for me to pet whenever I felt the need to pull hair, and my mother bought me a Persian kitten. That cat lived until last Christmas, outlasting my dear mom by four years.

"It's just the stress," I insisted. "I'm perfectly fine."

**ONCE OUR BOAT IS SAFELY DOCKED** at the bigger island, we start climbing the six hundred and sixty steps with the other people from our boat. Even as I struggle for breath after the first hundred steps, I am still craning my neck, on the lookout.

"Have to rest," I tell Jim. I grab onto a lichen-covered ledge for support and then sink down to rest on the edge of the stair.

"Are you all right?" he asks me. "You look pale."

"The boat," I say. "My stomach." I know I'm speaking cryptically but it's all I can manage.

I look back towards the boat and see that we are well ahead of one couple, both in their sixties, who came over with us. After a minute to calm my breathing, I ask Jim, "Think they'll make it?"

He looks down at them. "They told me they'd been training for this at home, in Boston."

I laugh. "For this?"

"It's important to them," Jim says. "He's got Irish blood."

"Me too," I say. "And, I was conceived because of Irish whiskey."

An observer would not notice Jim's change in expression, but I can see a wince, ever so slight. "Can we go now?" he asks. "We only have an hour and a half up here."

I reach for his hand. "Pull me," I say. "I'm just not as hardy as those crazy monks."

He takes my hand and we walk up the steps, slowly. How honeymoon-like. We walk at wedding-march speed.

**THE FINAL FIGHT BETWEEN MY FATHER AND JIM** was two years into the marriage. At best they were civil to each other; at worst, when Dad was drinking, words turned sharp and hurtful. On this particular night, my birthday dinner, my father had been drinking, of course, and the talk had turned to children. "Why isn't my little girl pregnant yet?" he said. "You got some problem with your willy?"

Jim took a sip of his coffee and said nothing.

"Eh?" my father said. "Eh? What good are you if you can't knock her up?"

"Dad," I said. "It's time for you to get going. I'll give you a lift home." I picked up his jacket and tried to hook my arm into his.

He shook me off. "I'm not going anywhere until he tells me what's wrong with him." He turned to look at Jim. "You think you're too important to have kids, is that it? He was referring to Jim's recent success in business, when his architectural firm had won a big design award. "Big man around town can't be bothered to make his wife happy?"

This was just after we found out that Jim was the problem. No, not Jim. Only his fertility. The morphology of his sperm was off, and we were doing all we could to remedy this. But despite wearing boxer shorts, ingesting massive amounts of Vitamin C and avoiding trans fats, nothing had changed.

Jim said to me, "I'm calling a cab." He reached for the phone. My father grabbed his arm.

"I'm not taking any cab, Mister President."

"You're not being reasonable. You're drunk. Maggie's not going to drive you, and neither am I." He reached for the phone again, and my father took a swing. Although it was a sloppy punch, it caught Jim's nose hard enough to spatter his shirt with blood. I grabbed a tea towel and held it to Jim's face.

"You don't tell me how to run my life, you artsy fag," my father said, shaking his fingers out.

"Dad!" I cried. "Can't you see what you've done?"

My father focused on my face. "What shoulda been done a long time ago."

"Get out," Jim said. "Now."

My father left then, walking out into the rainy night. I was angry, and ashamed, and sorry for Jim, whose pathology my tanked father had somehow divined.

"I can't do it any longer," he told me, once I was holding an ice pack to his face. "He's out of control."

"You're right," I said. "I hate it when he gets like this. But what can I do?"

"Stop having him here. Just draw the line. He's a sick man, Maggie. I don't think we can do anything for him, not anymore. We have to cut off contact."

I pictured what that might look like, just getting rid of a father. A gap in my life that big. But instead of feeling awful, it felt like a relief. I agreed to the plan.

Then, two years ago, he came into the clothing shop where I work. I didn't recognize his wasting body until he put his hand out to stop me. "My little girl," he said. "May God forgive me for what I have put you through." When I found out that he was sober, I was willing to talk. When I found out he was dying, I asked him to meet me for coffee. After months of treatments and surgeries and sombre predictions, he is still holding on, and still sober, and still Jim doesn't know I visit him.

Once he's dead, I will no longer be lying. Everything will return to how it should be, to how it was before our reunion.

Every day, I pray to my father's Catholic God to let him die.

**AFTER WE FINALLY MAKE IT TO THE TOP,** we wander around the beehive huts and Celtic crosses. The structures, made completely of stone, are round on the outside and rectangular on the inside, and it seems like rain would still not make it through the roofs of rock. Could anyone imagine a life here now, with no roads, no stores, no trees? I feel claustrophobic, just the same way I feel when I'm in the hospital visiting my father. Nowhere to turn for comfort.

I don't know how to tell Jim, or how he'd react if I did. Maybe in my head I have built this into something much bigger than it really is. After all, how could he ever turn away from one of his parents? His family is close; both parents are still healthy, married nearly fifty years, living at the same house for the last thirty. He would not dream of his life without them in it. He would understand where I'm coming from.

Except that I have kept it from him for too long. I had my chance— many chances—to break it to him right away, and I didn't. What is a marriage if the trust is gone? I'm afraid I have lost my "one more chance" card. This is not the first time I've kept a secret.

**THE MAN I HAD LUNCH WITH ONCE A MONTH WAS NOT A LOVER.** He was an old boyfriend, my first, in fact, someone from high school I had taken bubble baths with on winter days while his parents were cross-country skiing in the fields behind their house. We never slept together. I was a Catholic girl, deeply afraid of getting pregnant. Still, there was tenderness there, there was lust and frustration, with him excusing himself from the room after I'd worked him into a painful state. When we ran into each other at Kensington Market a few years ago with his four-year-old daughter, we planned a lunch date to catch up. At lunch he mentioned his divorce. He mentioned dreams of me, how he never stopped wondering what it would be like to "go all the way." He used the teenaged terminology, which made me laugh—and made a part of my brain wake up. What if this boyfriend got me pregnant this time around? Things would be different. Things would work out beautifully, if Jim never found out. I was thinking like a paperback heroine, desperate to be a mother then. I told the man we could meet again in a month, for lunch, but I still wasn't sure I could actually go through with something so devious. The month after that was when Jim walked into the café with his boss. It took me a long time to convince him that it was just lunch, which it still was, at that point. In my head, though, we had gone much further. I told Jim he could trust me. I was his wife. I loved him. It was true. I also wanted something he couldn't give me, and he knew that. Because of him coming into that café, and the look on his face when he saw me with another man, I never took the chance.

Now there he is, outside, marvelling at the stone construction, taking photos of crosses framed by the arches of the dwellings, trying to figure out how they put it all together without mortar. It strikes me here that we are engineers, too: we have made our lives work beautifully without children, thrown ourselves into pastimes like knitting and Irish history. Although I will still be in the running for another few years, we have made a kind of peace with all of that.

What I want now is a damned puffin.

I pull another hair from my head and run my fingers down its wavy length to find its root. It's a strange comfort, feeling the juiciness of the root, as if I am growing something that could be harvested and used, something to feed me, even though it has come from my own body. But I've broken the root off; there is nothing to feel at the end of the waves.

**AFTER WE DESCEND THE STONE STEPS** and endure another choppy two-hour boat ride back to the dock, during which Jim and the couple from Boston shout back and forth about the Celts, I want only to lie down. Once we're back in our Waterville B&B, Jim wraps me in a hug.

"I'm sorry about the timing," he tells me. "I wanted to see one too. Maybe there's some kind of zoo around here."

I stare at him. "A zoo?"

"You know, a reserve or some sort of thing like that."

I shake my head. "You think they would keep a puffin in a cage?"

"Hey, don't beat me up. I was just trying to help."

I touch him on the shoulder, gently. "I'm tired," I say. "I'm going to nap before dinner."

He gives me a head-tilt, our code.

I shake my head. He pats my shoulder.

"I'll take a walk, then," he says. "Meet me at the pub for dinner?"

I agree, and take my clothes off before crawling under the cool sheets. Jim's eyes linger on me, longing, I know, for more than a look. But all I can give him is a weak smile, with my eyes already closed.

While I nap, I dream of silverfish. The colour of dead skin, the bugs have become lodged in my scalp. When I run my fingers through my hair, my hands are covered in them. They race like water over my fingers, down my arms and into my mouth, and I wake myself up by screaming at the insects, which, in typical silverfish fashion, disappear into the cracks of dusky light.

**AT DINNER I SAY TO JIM, "I'M NOT DOING IT ANYMORE."**

"Doing what?"

"The trick," I say. "I'm done."

"Okay," Jim says, carefully. We have had versions of this conversation before. "But what do you mean, done? I thought it was more like, you know, an addiction. Once you're an addict, you're always—"

"Not for me. I will never do it again."

Jim smiles and reaches for my hand. "But how can you be so sure, Mags? I mean, you've been doing this a long time."

"I just know, that's all." If I mention that it came in a dream, he will laugh it off.

"How?"

"I just do!" I try to keep a cheerful, vacationy note in my voice but he's more persistent than usual.

"Is this, you know, hormonal?" He lowers his voice when he says it. I know he's trying to make sense of why I've kept turning him down since we arrived. And although he tells me he's not, I've seen him watching me when other men are around, trying to assess any attraction. But damn him for thinking things are hormonal, even when he's right most of the time.

"No, honey," I say. "Not everything is PMS."

If only it *were* PMS.

## THE NEXT MORNING, I WAKE UP WITH A HEADACHE.

"It *is* hormonal, isn't it?" Jim asks.

I play mute, with my arm pressed across my eyes. He quietly announces he is going to the common room to wait out the breakfast bell, and is careful to shut the door with the softest of clicks.

My head sometimes aches if I am too extreme with the hair pulling. A couple of strands, though, seem to relieve the pressure, a kind of blood-letting I have come to rely upon. I run my fingers over my scalp. I might have been yanking at my hair all night in my sleep. Near the back of my head there is a small patch of bristles, a garden of new sprouts coming up. That's the place I turned to when my father was very sick, his most recent turn for the worst. Somehow, he stabilized once again, and gave me the go-ahead to carry on with the trip.

My father and I have become cautiously closer during the two years, with him telling stories about his childhood and tales of adventure abroad that leave me shaking my head. I don't talk much about my life, although he wants me to. Jim's a good man, he keeps telling me, shaking his head. I was a drunken blind man for too many years to see it. When the opportunity for the trip came up, he insisted. Go on, he said. Go kiss the Blarney Stone for me, not that I need any more gift of the gab. Go see the puffins. All those years of boozing hadn't taken away what my father could give me: a generosity of spirit, a parent's simple, unwavering love for their child.

My fingers keep roaming through my hair. No one would be the wiser if I just took a couple more. But Jim's words come back to me. *Long-term addiction.* I am going cold turkey. I sit up in bed and heave the heavy feather duvet off my legs. Enough, I say, as I did in my dream. Puffins or not, headache or not, I am not going to remove another hair from my aching head.

**AFTER BREAKFAST,** Jim and I decide to follow through on our original plans and rent bicycles and ride to Sneem. Because it's nearly fifty kilometres along the Kerry coast and I have never ridden more than an hour anywhere, we will take the bus back to Waterville at the end of the day. A few miles from Sneem, there is an ancient ruin called Staigue Fort that Jim would love to visit. I want him to see it. I want him to be happy. Sneem is also the town my father worked in, for a few months, at a luxury hotel that catered to American celebrities and wealthy Europeans. I haven't bothered bringing up this fact.

We fill our daypacks with fruit and buns, cheese and water, and set off. Five minutes after we start cycling, the road rises. *May the road rise to meet you.* I repeat the Irish blessing in my head as I work my way through the gears until I am at the easiest. After another five minutes, I pull my bike off the road and stop beside a stone fence.

"Jim," I call. "Jim!" He is too far ahead to hear me. My calves are cramping, and the back of my throat feels scorched. I should have trained for Ireland like the Bostonian couple did. I get off my bike and sit down on the fence, which is wide and short and made of piled stones, and drink half of my water in one draw.

"Jim!" I call again. But he is still pedalling. He is such a—I don't know what he is. An eager beaver? A selfish cad? Many options fly through my head. But are any of them appropriate for this man who has come to this old, rocky country, ready for whatever I might throw his way? And he doesn't even know the half of it. I am fooling him, every minute of every day.

So he is a fool.

No. Not him. If anyone is a fool—

But names don't matter, for there he is, turning around after only a minute, coasting back down the hill he has just climbed. He is just my husband, no other names needed.

"Mags," he calls. "What's wrong?"

I shake my head. "I just needed a rest."

"Already?" He is breathing heavily, but no more than he does at the tennis courts back home.

"If you want to go on without me, go ahead."

"What are you talking about?" he asks. "I'm not going anywhere without you." "I can't make it," I say. "I want to go. I do. But not like this."

Jim gets off his bike. He leans it against the fence before wiping the sweat from his forehead with his sleeve. "Shall we take the bus both ways, then, Maggie?" He is getting exasperated: he always starts talking very slowly, very calmly, as if he is underwater. It's his method, to pretend he isn't bothered by my silliness: silliness is my word, but I know he would use it if he could. He talks to me as if I am mad, or have a gun in my hand, like Rolph in the Sound of Music, which we

THE JEALOUSY BONE

watched last night with our hosts at the B&B, saying he'll shoot but gradually giving into the soothing voice of Captain Von Trapp.

"A bus," I say, massaging my calves. "I think that might be best."

Jim nods. Then he sits down beside me on the fence and stares out at the field. "This was all trees," he says, after a minute of clear green silence. "We are sitting in a clearcut."

I examine the fields around us, up and down the hills, fenced in haphazard fashion. "Tell me again why we're here," I say. "We could've vacationed in a clearcut closer to home. Taken a day trip to Temagami, or gone across the country to BC."

I am trying for humour, but I brace myself for another slow response. What am I doing, playing with him like this? I can't help it. My hands race through my hair, seeking thickness, a strand with girth I can tug upon and not remove. I think of my father in his bed, how I brushed his hair during our last visit. How he told me to grab a hold of a chunk of his hair and pull, something he used to ask me to do when I was a kid. No matter how hard I pulled, it didn't hurt him. I was afraid, in the hospital, but after he insisted he could take it, I pulled his hair. It was still true. I pulled with all my strength, and he couldn't feel it, and none of his wiry grey hair came out. The rest of his body was failing him, but he would die with a full head of hair.

Jim doesn't say anything. He simply nods again and we sit in silence, gazing out at the divided green land. It hits me here: I am in the process of giving the trip to him. No puffins, what do I care? So we might not make it to Sneem. So what? I don't want to lead anymore, or have my priorities come first. I will be a tag-along. In fact, giving the trip to him is the least I can do.

"We can't let the bikes go to waste," I say. "Isn't there an easier place to go?"

"I'm sure we can find somewhere," Jim says, turning to look at me. "Thank you."

"For what?"

"For bringing me here." He motions towards the fields, and the ocean beyond, where we can just make out the faint, ship-like shapes of the Skelligs.

"I didn't—"

"Yes, you did." He puts his arm around me. "I'm having a marvellous time in this clearcut. And look," he says, pointing with his other hand. "There's a little ring fort right over there." I can make out a circle of stones, sinking into the wet green land.

His arm is trapping my hair as he presses me to his shoulder. It isn't against the agreement if someone else does the pulling. I close my eyes. I ease my head gently away. I'm not like my father: it hurts.

I look at Jim's face, run my gaze down his nose, follow the ridge that veers slightly from centre, then back into line. What Jim is, is a decent man. My loyalty should have remained with him.

**BACK IN WATERVILLE,** we ask about easier day trips. We decide to bus to Caherciveen, because of the hills, and from there we will take our bikes on a ferry to Valencia Island, a place neither of us knows anything about. On the island, we come upon a nature interpretation centre called The Skellig Experience, made for tourists out looking for authenticity but not up for the real thing, and because we are hot from cycling—more hills here—and curious about what we might find, we decide to check it out. The air inside is blessedly frigid. I can feel sweat trickling through my hair, and the silverfish dream comes back to me, making me shudder.

"Too cold?" Jim asks.

"No, it's perfect," I say. "Just a bit of a shock."

Replicas of the beehive huts stand beside tableaux of the monks harvesting fish from the benevolent sea. Sea birds are frozen in

THE JEALOUSY BONE

flight, their cries piping in from mesh circles on the wall. It might have impressed us a few days ago, but Jim and I have seen all of this first-hand.

"Kind of pales in comparison," Jim says. "I'm glad we went for ourselves."

I agree, although I let my eyes wander, quietly searching out the puffin display. Jim was right, after all. This isn't a zoo, but it's as close as we are going to get. Against the far wall, I spot the exhibit.

The mannequin in front of me is not real in any sense of the word. I can't believe they exist like this in the wild. I know puffins look absurd, but this? This is a large starling with a plastic mask. This is a silly Halloween disguise. The beak looks like a crab's pincer, with a yellow hinge where the bottom and top connect, and it seems like it would pull the bird over with its weight. How it manages to fly at all without plummeting head-first into the Irish Sea is a mystery like the flight of bumblebees.

I press the button beside the artificial puffin. The sound that comes out is more cow than bird, a low mooing that makes a quack sound musical. Who could ever dream of such a creature? Why do these natural absurdities even exist in the world? I push the button again.

No beauty without its counterpart. No joy without sorrow. The Catholic morality from childhood returns, here, in the land of religious division, in The Skellig Experience. But what of crosses to bear? And what, if I get down to the basics, of forgiveness? I have taken my father back into my life, however hidden and particular the parameters, not because he asked for it, or because I had to unburden my heart, but simply because he is sick, and dying, and I didn't know what else to do. He is my father, from birth until death; the vows that Jim and I exchanged, the bad blood between them, neither of these can change the facts.

Jim comes over eventually, curious about the sound. He stands behind me and wraps his arms around my waist. "Was that a sea cow?" he asks, nuzzling my neck and kissing me just below the ear.

"No," I say, and let myself relax against him. "That was my puffin."

"Will you look at that." He is staring at the fake bird, perched on a piece of driftwood. "That's one funny-looking bird."

"Phantasmagorical is not what I'd call it."

"Phantasma *who?*"

"Oh, it's just how my father used to describe it."

"Ah," he says. "Well, we won't tell him what we think." Jim laughs. "If the old bastard's still alive, what he doesn't know won't hurt him."

I tense up beneath Jim's hands, then relax so he won't ask questions. But my mind is plagued with questions. Is our marriage strong enough to weather the truth? Will he ever believe me again? Will he be there for me, down the road, when the children we don't have won't be there to brush my hair in the hospital, if I have any left?

"Jim," I say, turning around to face him. "Let's go back to the B&B."

"What?" he asks. "What is it?"

I tilt my head and smile. "There's something we need to do." I run my hand up the inside of his leg, under his shorts, until I am touching the soft skin of his upper thigh.

Jim pulls me closer and kisses me deeply, while the plastic puffin watches. I let myself feel the kisses. He loves me. This is a honeymoon. This is what we came for.

"We're going to get kicked out of here," Jim whispers. "Unless we sneak into that beehive hut." He takes me by the wrist and gently pulls me towards the display.

"Let's wait," I say, smiling, resisting his pull. "I want us to take our time." I will tell Jim everything, soon enough. Right now I just want to enjoy the honeymoon. I point at my helmet looped around his wrist. "Shall we?"

"All right." He sighs. "Although I wish to God we didn't have to go anywhere."

"It's always faster on the way back."

"True enough." He hands me my helmet. "Not that you need this," he says. "We only saw about ten cars the whole time."

I put it on and fasten it under my chin. At least my head, and the hair upon it, will be safe for as long as it takes to ride back to the ferry dock.

Then I remember. "Wait," I say to Jim, who's already out the door. "I forgot something." I turn back to the display cabinets and pull out my camera. I won't be able to fool myself, but to a nearly blind man, this will look like the real thing.

# FALSE SPRING

**WHILE LEAH IS OUT WALKING,** and their son, Toby, is at school, Marcus watches the purple finches at the near-empty feeder in their backyard. Every so often his fingers rise off his armrests and flutter before landing again. Red onions are purple. Purple finches are red. His mind is stuck on this conundrum, a sleeve caught in barbed wire, a leg in a trap. The sun on his skin is no comfort today, even though they have been whining about the weather for weeks. He knows it won't last; he's not going to let himself get used to it.

He wheels himself back inside the house.

Leah walks along the side streets, her outer thighs brushing the silky lining of her coat. Her inner thighs slide past each other, lightly powdered, so as not to chafe. It's February 13th in Victoria. Everyone is wearing a smile. Leah is wearing only her pink velvet coat and a black-haired wig.

She thinks she can feel stares gathering on her back, feels them through the velvet, oscillating, like invisible ants, as she walks through the city. There is nothing between her skin and their eyes

82

but that coat. The ornamental cherry blossoms create a pale perfume, millions of blossoms concentrating their focus into one small whiff of spring. She is lonely. She is happy. She is not Leah, not for at least another three hours, when she has to pick up her son from school.

**JAY FIDDLES WITH THE TEA TOWELS** on the stove handle and rereads the message on his fridge. *Running away brings you home.* He can't take his focus off the sentence. It's rearrangeable, too, but once these phrases are written he never moves them. He has others, in straight lines, from handle to hinge. *Trees touch the earth and eat from shadows. You can see inside my song.* CBC is drifting its net of words down over the fridge, bombings in Iraq, new Prime Minister follies, farmers angry over mad cows. This irony amuses Jay. But, right now, he is meditating on the fridge koan. *Running away brings you home.* He didn't write it. He lives alone. The only other person to have been this close to his fridge is Ann, his yoga therapist, and she doesn't come to play with magnets. If she did, her words might be more like: *Running away is futile. Embrace the pain.*

He looks around the apartment. From where he is in the kitchenette, he can see everything but the bathroom. It's nearly as big as the rest of the apartment, a deep claw foot tub, a toilet with a round tank, a checkerboard tile floor, big enough for a party. He can't really imagine what that might look like. He hasn't had a party since he was a kid, back in Manitoba, farm kids gathered around a kitchen table, eating angel food cake.

This bachelor is a sublet, a home along the way to finding where he's meant to be. He's looking for a feel. Resonance. Ever since his only serious girlfriend broke it off, four years ago, after telling him he wasn't deep enough to marry, he's been methodically changing locations every year, an experiment in transience that has left him with foldable furniture and very few friends. Most jobs, unlike girl-friends, are easier to come by than most people think. You just need to set your standards low enough, have a skill that's in high demand, and keep people happy enough to make them good references for the future. So far, so good. Every city needs another computer tech. Other than work, he tells himself that he doesn't need much. He's like an epiphyte, one of those frizzy green air plants from the '70s. Very little needed to keep him alive.

When Jay asks himself if it was his own hand compiling, con-necting letters in the dark while he slept, he doesn't answer. It's his cardinal rule. If you live alone and talk aloud, you're lonely. If you answer your own questions, you're done for. No one else could have written it. Is this the resonance he's been waiting for? he wonders. Is this divine? Is this a sign that someone, something, has been in his space, infiltrating his musings, giving him a message that this might be the place to land?

He gives his head a shake. Damned coast is getting to him. What he wants is to dive into his duvet and sleep. Instead he does his stretches, for Ann, for his bad lower back, and thinks about his grocery list. She's trying to get him to cut out sugar this month, for the clarity of mind it will bring. So far he's just grumpier than normal. He should ask her if it will make him deeper. Or if it might make him sleepwalk and write weird things on his fridge.

## LAST WEEK, MARCUS BROUGHT UP LEAH'S WALK while she was cooking. She was making risotto, adding the broth to the rice every few minutes.

Marcus was sitting in his wheelchair by the patio doors. "I know about your walks. The wig, the coat."

Leah looked at him, tried to catch his eye. He was staring at the rain hitting the window. He kept his eyes on the wet glass.

"It's a bit weird," he said. "But I don't mind. I want you to have a life. And happiness."

"I have a life," she said. "With you and Toby."

Marcus let his head drop forward. "You wouldn't go out like that if you were happy." Leah walked over to him and squeezed his shoulders, then kissed the top of his head.

"I've only done it twice," she said. "I can't explain it. It just came over me. But if you want me to stop, I will."

Marcus cranked his head around to look at her. "No. It's time. I want you to find someone."

She stared at him.

"To sleep with."

Leah shook her head. "I can't do that."

"I want you to be happy."

"Marcus, I am—"

"Happier than this!" Marcus flung his hands out towards the kitchen, then down towards his lower half. "Don't tell me that this is enough anymore. I'm not going to believe you."

"Marcus," she said. "I love you. I want to be with you. I don't need to be with someone else. Sometimes I just need to *be* someone else for an hour or so."

Marcus looked at his feet. "Don't we all."

She had to go back to the stove and stir in another cup of broth. The rice couldn't be left alone for more than three minutes, or it would burn. If Toby wasn't so hooked on video games, he would be standing on a chair beside her with a wooden spoon, keeping the grains from sticking to the pot. She heard the Super Mario song from the living room intensify. Mario was fighting another Boss. If Marcus hadn't bought him the damned system, she might be able to get a little help around the house. But what else can Marcus and Toby do together, that might bring them as much fun? She had no right to complain.

Marcus wheeled over to her side. His cheeks were wet. "I'm not asking you to tell me about it. I just want to know that you're being loved."

Leah rummaged through her bags of spices, looking for the rosemary. "I don't even have enough time to put these into jars. You think I have enough time for anything else?"

"I know you have time to walk around naked," he said in a low voice. "How much time do you need?"

"I'm not naked," she said. But he had already wheeled himself into the living room, to help their son fight the forces of evil.

**"IT'S ABOUT TAKING RISKS,"** Ann tells Jay. "Taking the plunge. When your muscles shake like that, you're really getting into the pose." Ann makes house calls. Jay has been sitting in office chairs for too many years, and he knows that yoga helps, but he can't manage the classes in this city, the uniform of tight pants and bare arms even men are supposed to wear. He found Ann's ad in the yellow pages, to "privately unwind his spine." It had a slightly sexual tone to it, the unwinding in private, but when Jay phoned to book an appointment, her voice mail message made it clear he wasn't the only one who'd wondered at the descriptor. "If you're looking for anything other than therapeutic exercise, I suggest you look elsewhere," it said. Jay left a voice mail. That's all he wanted. From her, at least.

"Is it supposed to hurt so much?" Jay asks now, grimacing in Triangle pose.

"It's the nectar of the asana. The centre. Let go of your preconceived notions about what is normal." Ann has his head in her hands, turning it slowly to loosen his neck. "Normal is simply what the lazy have made common."

One of Jay's vertebrae clicks into place. "What was that?" he asks.

"A good sign," Ann says. "Focus on your breathing."

"Do you do that to all your victims?"

"Only the ones who complain too much." Ann says. This is a rare stab at humour. Ann is all business, despite earrings made of Fimo and sparkly beads. Her grey hair rises in spikes from her head, as if every hair is standing in Mountain pose, an imaginary string pulling each strand towards the sky.

When Jay has finished the standing poses, Ann tells him to lie down. "Shivasana," she says. "Pose of the corpse." Jay lies on his back on a fleece throw and slows his breathing and shuts his eyes. Story time. This is what Jay pays for. The postures are all well and good, and they've helped him out already, but Ann's words seem to influence his life more than loose pectorals. Every session, it's a different story, something to absorb into the body like sunlight. Ann begins her tale, after her Om thins into silence. As instructed, Jay pretends to be dead.

"I have a friend," she intones as she walks around Jay, "who knows the meaning of letting go better than anyone else I've ever met. She has a difficult life, by our standards: a disabled husband, in a wheel-chair, a young child, a hard time keeping food on the table. But when she's had enough of the role she's in, she goes walking around the city. Now this may not seem to be much of a departure. So she takes a walk. So what? But the other day, for the second time this year, she went walking in nothing but a pink velvet coat. Nothing beneath it except her skin."

Jay's eyes open.

"You're interested," she says. "The goal of meditation is to remain detached from the thoughts sliding through your mind."

Jay's eyes quickly close.

"She wasn't out there soliciting," Ann says. "Unless she was so-liciting a new self for those few hours. Someone removed from the tedium of laundry and chasing down health insurance. A woman who could be anyone she wants. She wore a hat and glasses, in case she was recognized. The first day she did it, she wore a wig. But both days, along with the coat, she carried that desire to let go of who she was at home."

"I want you do that here, Jay. Can you free yourself of identity, of attachment, of a label? Can you recreate a new self, a simple, inner self that will be able to bounce back from anything that might come your way?"

Jay's eyes are still closed. But his mind is opening. He wants to know how long the coat is. Where she walks. If her injured husband can still get it up.

**MARCUS AND LEAH** met seven years ago, on the beach, right after he had peeled himself out of a 6 millimetre wetsuit. She was reading, sheltered by a driftwood structure that people slept in at night. It was spring, and sunny, and her shoulders were bare except for the goose bumps.

"You mind if I leave this here while I take a run?" he asked, holding up his dripping wetsuit. The guys he'd been windsurfing with had taken the rest of his gear.

Leah did mind. She didn't want to have to worry about anything. But once she saw his black hair, all gloss and curl and bounce, she heard herself saying yes.

"Cool," he said. "Be back in half an hour."

She kept her eyes on her paragraph but listened as he ran up the beach towards Clover Point, where kites chased their tails in the off-shore breeze. She could hear his footsteps above the waves, digging into the smooth stones at a furious pace. Only when she couldn't hear them did she turn to watch him, chopping into those rocks and somehow moving forward while everyone else on the beach struggled to stay upright. His curls jumped with every stride.

After this meeting it was a dangerously quick slide into co-habitation. Pregnant before the end of summer. Baby Toby the following spring.

When the diving accident downed him with an incomplete spinal cord injury, it was like a plug pulled from a socket. No power to the muscles that used to kite-surf, scuba dive, or rock-climb. For months, adventure took on a new meaning: getting the spoon from bowl to mouth.

Now, after two years, he can use the top half of his body; the line has been drawn just above the waist of his drawstring pants. Now, this is Leah's life, married to a man who can't walk unless she presses him against her chest from behind, scooping him out of his wheelchair by holding under his armpits. She waits until he makes the first move. Left foot, big step, right foot, small. A lopsided dance they do across the dining room floor, marking the space where a table should be. This is what their love is. Keeping the blood flowing. Keeping what movement there is from vanishing. Keeping the possibilities alive.

Toby is six. He watches them take their stilted journey from window to kitchen and back again; he tells Leah he wants to know how to do it when he gets older. He gets an allowance every week to make sure his toys are kept out of the way. "This is a tidy sum," Marcus says every time he hands Toby the toonie. Toby's just starting to get jokes, and now he's starting to tell Marcus some from school. What do you call a man with no arms and legs by the front door? he asked once. Marcus still laughed at that one, even though once Toby realized what he was saying, he went red in the face. Matt.

It didn't apply to Marcus. He had everything. Half of it just wasn't working.

**AS SHE'S ROLLING UP HER MAT,** Ann mentions the yoga retreat she'll be taking some of her students on in a few weeks.

"We're going to Mexico for ten days," she says to Jay. "You could use the Vitamin D."

"I'll think about it," he says. He will think about it. The thought will circulate like a mosquito hawk, alight in the corners of his mind, and wait to eat all the pesty other thoughts through the days ahead. But Jay avoids the grocery store at 5 pm. He orders Swiss Chalet delivery. When small children run towards him on the sidewalk, he jumps onto the grass, scowling. A trip to a foreign country makes no sense at all.

Still, he asks her: "What kind of people are going?"

"Oh, the usual group of middle-aged women, plus a journalist and a few younger people. Nice folks. No one too trendy."

What harm would it do him to check it out? "I'll let you know."

"Don't wait too long," Ann says. "I only have a few places left."

**LEAH PASSES THROUGH CHINATOWN** and steals a lychee fruit. She balances on the train tracks. Only three short trains use it every day. She walks to the wall where a mural of whales is painted: the whaling wall. An absurd number of orcas breach and roll in the cracked turquoise paint, while the harbour beside the wall is littered with sea planes and kayaks. The ferry on the far side is taking on tourists, to transport them back across the border with their exchange rate bargains and maple syrup. I could board that ship, she thinks. I could be over there in ten minutes, run on with the last of the cars. She forgets for a moment that it is no longer easy to cross the border. With what she's disguising under her coat, it would be easier to swim across.

If I'm going to do this, it has to happen naturally, Leah thinks. I'm not going through the classifieds, or any blind dates, or set-ups. It has to happen on its own, if it happens at all. She imagines another lover. How it would feel to have someone above her, or kneeling behind her, or standing up, with him inside of her. God, she misses Marcus. A private joke to only her from when it first happened—she either cried or laughed when she thought of it—comes back into her head: Would the old Marcus please stand up?

If it happens, he has to look completely different from Marcus. She starts to picture what that would look like: reddish hair, on the thin side, thin lips, blue eyes, delicate hands. A quiet man, searching, like her, for something outside of himself. All limbs working. All parts moving.

She starts looking at the people on the sidewalks, and immediately feels like a vulture. A trained vulture. A vulture allowed to hunt when it's not sure it's even hungry, once the instinct has been buried.

But she keeps on looking.

**JAY IS SOAKING IN THE DEEP OVAL TUB** in his giant bathroom. He's finished with Ann for today. Pieces of flaked paint from the sides of the tub float around his body like peeled skin. The window is open and he can smell the ocean. Last month he heard sea lions off shore, barking nearly every night. The males come up from Baja California to fatten up for the females, who join them later. They have their own island, just beyond the highest-priced real estate in the city. The Oak Bay residents complain about the noise. According to the paper, they've called the police in more than once.

Jay misses the sound of the sea lions, hints of the time they must be having, lounging around in the sun, eating as much as they can handle, and travelling only if they feel so inclined. He wonders when the females will get here, what that will sound like; if he'll recognize the difference, or if they'll make any sound at all.

**WHEN LEAH GETS TO DALLAS ROAD,** she stops to stare at the Olympic Mountains across the strait. The snow-capped tops and the folds of their forested slopes are oddly illuminated today, and make them seem close enough to touch. By the end of the summer only the highest ridge will still be white. Hurricane Ridge. She was there before, with Marcus and Toby, when Toby was just learning to walk. They walked around on the grainy snow in shorts and sandals, threw handfuls at each other, watched as it turned to water in their hands. They camped at the foot of the mountains beside a clear blue glacial lake and swam, shrieking, the water barely changed from solid to liquid.

She wishes she could see her life, the whole thing, the way she can see the ridge of mountains across the Strait. If she could see it all laid out, the timeline, the peaks and valleys... Such an obvious metaphor for a marriage but what else does she have? If she could see it all, then she might know what step to take next, what logic might actually exist where it feels like only chaos.

She wants to be as temporary as ice. Like a snowball, or a piece of ice shipped from the lagoons of Iceland to a bar in Japan, a thousand years of untold history melting into a cola. That desirable; that fleeting; that untraceable.

A man with a chocolate lab smiles at her when she looks at his dog, chasing its tail. She nods, and walks away in a way that she hopes is not enticing in the least. Too soon for any of this. Much too soon.

Is that why she's blushing?

**ANN HAS KNOWN MARCUS AND LEAH** for years, ever since Leah took a prenatal yoga class with her. Now she is helping Marcus with modified asanas, focusing on the first and second chakras. Wear orange and red boxers, she's advised him. Bring the heat back into the furnace. She's there when Leah gets home from walking. While Marcus is meditating, Leah takes her into the bathroom to show off the new shower curtain she bought on her walk, a sidewalk sale at a hardware store. It's covered with starfish and anemones, little blue and yellow fish.

"It makes me think of Mexico," Ann says. "I'm leading a retreat there next month."

"Ann," Leah says. "He wants me to find someone. He won't let it go."

"He told me," she says quietly. "What do you think?"

"He told you?" Leah looks into the mirror and studies her nose. "I think it's crooked," she says.

"He wants you to be happy."

Leah's peering closely at her nose. "I know. This thing has never been the same since my surgery."

"You can repair cartilage, you know," Ann says. "I'll give you some affirmations. Blue-green algae works, too. But what about it?"

Leah sighs. "It feels like he's pushing me." She hangs a wet sweater over the shower curtain rod, pulling back the new curtain to keep the black dye away from it.

"What happens if you don't?"

"Nothing." Leah kneels and starts scrubbing the bathtub with baking soda. "And if you do?"

Leah stops scrubbing. "I think—I'm afraid of liking it. I'm afraid of what I'll find. But how can it compare to what he, what we—." She turns to look at Ann. "We had an amazing sex life. We didn't even have to try."

Ann nods. "But is there anything wrong with liking it?"

"Aside from bad karma? And a little boy named Toby?" Leah turns on the tap and rinses the dirt away. "I'm not sure I could look either of them in the eye again."

"Do you have anyone in mind? I mean, not that I'm assuming you're going to do it, but I know a few—"

"No," she says. "But thank you. I want to find him on my own."

Ann grins suddenly. "I have an idea," she says. "Why don't you come with me to Mexico? You'd have to get right on it, though. I only have two more spots, and this morning's client is thinking it over."

Leah goes back to the mirror and re-examines her face. "I've got too much sun damage already," she says. "I'm starting to show my sins."

"Get a sombrero. They're big enough to camp under, and they sell them right on the beach."

"I'll think about it." She turns away from the mirror and puts her hand on Ann's arm. "It's not about penetration, you know. Just for a little while, I want to lose this sense of responsibility."

"He wants you to be satisfied."

"I know," Leah says. "That's the problem. He satisfies me, as best as he can. But I don't always want to come out of pity."

**WHEN JAY GETS OUT OF HIS BATH,** he lies on his futon and wraps himself in an old quilt. He's not in the mood to lie there; every time he starts to meditate, that woman in her pink coat floats into his reverie.

He pulls on some clothes and takes a walk. It feels like he has twenty pairs of eyes burning from his head, Mag-Lites lighting up every corner of the city. Pink coat. Pink coat. There are very few pink coats. None of them are velvet. The only velvet coat he sees is brown and white, like cowhide, at the coffee shop he's taken his forty eyes to, to keep watch. The woman inside the coat looks at him. She's got two silver studs jutting out below her lower lip, like extra teeth. She gives him a movie script look, as if she can see herself in all of his eyes, like a wall of televisions. Jay turns away and watches his coffee swirl. When he looks back up, she's still staring.

True to what his ex called his antisocial nature, he hates coffee shops. Especially ones that seem to inspire customers to say Gracias instead of thank you. Regulars with dirty hair and free newspapers. Receptionists in jean skirts, watching the clock. Writers hooking their left hands over their notebook pages, to protect the newly discovered truth. Is this the kind of depth my girlfriend wanted? he asks himself. And, am I really here to find this velvet-cloaked woman? But of course, he doesn't answer.

What he does know is that he's ready for a change, even after only a few months in this city. Island-bound. Lonely. Horny. Tired of another daily grind.

Maybe he will go to Mexico. Maybe it is time to let go of the old him, shed that skin for the new person inside. Running away brings you home, the fridge says. Is home what he's looking for? Or is he just looking to get laid?

**AFTER DINNER, TOBY AND LEAH SIT** at the kitchen table playing Snakes and Ladders and eating cinnamon hearts.

"What would you think if I went for a little trip?" she asks him, and counts out eleven spaces.

"Can I come?" he asks. "Where are you going?"

"Here," she says and hands him the dice. "Mexico."

He rolls them onto the board and sends both of their markers flying. "I want to come with you."

"Watch what you're doing," she says, sharply. Then, softer, "It's adults only."

"But who's gonna watch me?" He looks up at her with his eyes wide.

Leah laughs. "Your father, silly."

"But he's an adult," Toby replies. "He'll want to go with you."

Leah holds the dice out to Toby again. "Try again," she says. "But this time, do it gently."

Toby shakes the two dice in his hands slowly, then opens his palms just wide enough for them to slip through. "Seven," he says, and counts his marker over seven spaces. "No fair," he says. "I have to go all the way back down." He slides his marker down the back of a snake, then drops his head.

"Do you want to stop the game?" Leah asks. "We don't have to play."

"Mexico is dumb," he says. "I think you should stay here."

Leah nods her head slowly, looking at Toby's unwashed hair. She touches his crown before shaking the bag of candy beside her. "Do you know what we used to do with these?"

She pulls a candy from the bag of hearts and licks it, then rubs it over her lips. "Now give me your hand." She brings the back of his small hand to her lips and presses them against the skin.

"Look," she says.

But he's looking at her face, not his hand. "You look pretty."

Marcus wheels himself into the kitchen. "What's that about pretty?"

"Mommy looks pretty. Look at her lips."

Marcus looks at Leah as she shakes the dice and throws them onto the board. "Yes, she does."

"It's not my colour," Leah says. She is shocked to find herself blushing, again. She moves her man three spaces, then hands Marcus the bag of candy. "Here, have some. I've had more than my share."

"So?" Marcus asks. "You're thinking about it?"

"Oh, I don't know. It's in three weeks. That's too soon."

"Yoga in Mexico? Sounds pretty nice."

"But it's too expensive, and we—"

"We can make it. It'll be your birthday and Christmas present."

"Ha. For the next five years."

"I can do yoga," Toby says. He lies on the floor and spreads his legs and arms wide open. "We do this at school. I'm a starfish."

Leah laughs. "I wish you could come, buddy, but it's not for kids."

"Go, honey."

"I'll think about it." She smiles. "That's something, isn't it?" She bends down and kisses Marcus on the lips.

"Be careful, Snow White," he says. "Those ruby lips might rub off." He pulls her down to sit sideways on his lap.

"Be careful," she says, quietly. "I'm heavy."

He wraps his arms around her. "It's all right. I know what I can handle."

"Girl germs! Girl germs!" Toby yells, and runs into the living room, back to another video game.

**JAY PARTS THE MOSQUITO NET** and lies down on his bed, gazing up at the white mesh that looks like a snowfall that will never touch him. He does a mock snow angel with his arms and legs and thinks about growing up in Winnipeg. He remembers how hard it was to come out of that position and not wreck the angel, and how he wanted to be picked up by a crane, hoisted right out of that snow straight up, so his perfect imprint would remain.He closed his eyes and thought more of snow, to stop thinking of Leah. Once they were finished dinner the first night, Ann pulled him aside and told him that she was the coat woman, but to not tell anyone that he knew. Who would he tell, exactly?

**LEAH'S ROOM HAS A BIRD MOTIF**; there are painted wood carvings of tropical birds, a painting of a hummingbird above the bed, and small birds circling over her head in a mobile as she lies on her back, waiting for a breeze to come in through the small windows.

It's siesta time, and she should be tired. Only two days into the trip and most people in the group are fighting the heat and the intense yoga with long naps. But Leah is wide awake, thinking of Jay. When she saw him at the airport, he smiled at her. When she saw he was one of only two men on the journey, she had to fight back fear and anger and yes, desire. He fits the bill: all four quadrants of his body function. He has light red hair. The hands of a pianist. Eyes that are almost the same blue as her own. He's travelling alone.

Now, after partnering up with him for the two-person stretches, feeling his back against hers as they sat spine to spine for the last pose of the morning, she can feel that attraction wanting to pull her outside her casita and walk across the courtyard to Jay's little house. He's doing what she's doing, avoiding the hottest part of the day, doing what the locals do. Traditional. They are following tradition.

Is taking a lover as prescribed by your husband traditional?

Her body thrums with that word: lover. It's been a long time since another man has touched her—not by golden anniversary standards but long enough to find the whole thing, the idea of the thing, alluring. Frightening. Like jumping off the cliff at that glacial lake, its freezing blue water below.

She has to forget that Marcus wants this. She does not want to report back, make notes, lie in bed with him and recap. If there is anything to recap. She might be fooling herself entirely, here. Jay might be gay. He might not want her. He might think she's a brazen hussy, walking over to his casita in her sundress that hugs all the places she wants him to touch.

She likes the way it moves against her skin as she walks beneath the bougainvillea, arching over Jay's door.

Jay is almost asleep when he hears the knock. He sits up and calls out, Hello?

"It's Leah," she says from behind the door.

"Come in, come in," he says. He sits up and rubs his face to wake himself up.

She walks in and sees him behind the netting. "Oh, I'm sorry," she says. "Were you sleeping?"

"No, just resting."

She smiles. "Are the mosquitoes bad in here?"

Jay blushes. "Ah, no. Just being cautious."

"I like it." She sits on the edge of the bed, on the outside of the net. "Quite exotic."

"Come in," he says, then tries to find the opening. He gets on his knees and works his way around the whole thing until he is in front of her, sweeping the net to find the separation.

She stops him by grabbing his hand. "Watch," she says, and pulls the edge up from the bottom and ducks under it. "Voila."

For a moment she is acutely aware of what the white netting looks like, veiling her head. He sees it too, but thankfully, he says nothing.

"Welcome," he says. "Siesta time?"

"Okay."

They lie down, side by side, on their backs.

"This is my favourite yoga pose," he says. "Shivasana."

Leah laughs. "It's nice after our morning."

Ann had them up before 7 am to do sun salutations, then two more hours of asanas after breakfast, in a palm grove by the ocean.

"That's Ann for you." Jay's heart is pounding harder than it was after the salutations. "Still glad you came?"

"God, yes."

"Needed a break?"

"You could say that."

They are quiet for a few moments before Jay says, "Leah, I know more about you that I've let on."

She sits up. "What do you know? How do you know?"

"Ann."

He tells her what she told him, about the walks, the coat, the injured husband. He doesn't say anything about sanctioned lovers. At least Ann has kept that much to herself.

"You're so brave," Jay says.

"Ha! Not me."

"You are. All I do is give up when the going gets rough."

Leah turns to face him. "What are you running from?"

He shrugs. "Heartache. Boredom. Bad weather. Same old same old."

"A restless soul," Leah says, dramatically.

"Yeah. Something like that."

She takes his hand in both of hers. "Your fingers. They're lovely."

He doesn't say anything while she traces each finger with her index finger, in and out along their edges. He wants her to keep doing that forever, he wants her to look at him, to kiss him. He wants her. He's wanted her since the story Ann told him.

He takes his hand back and touches her face. She doesn't tell him to stop.

It's after, when they're lying spooned into each other, that Leah begins to cry. It's when she becomes aware of Jay's foot, tracing her calf, and his thigh pressing into her own, that she remembers why she is here, of what she has lost.

Jay holds her while she cries. 'I can't promise anything," she says. 'I'm sorry."

"I haven't asked you to." He kisses her shoulder. "This is enough for me. Right now."

"Are you a Buddhist?"

'No," he says, laughing. "Why?"

"You have that way about you. A presence. Some kind of calmness."

"I'm working on it. Non-attachment."

Leah turns around, quickly. "That's it. That's what I need."

Jay laughs. "Okay, then."

She kisses him. They have their siesta. They move on through the rest of the retreat, making love and stretching their bodies until they shake. While the surf pounds in front of them, while they drink margaritas in the small Mexican town, they practice being in the moment, staying present, existing only here and now.

**LEAH DOESN'T TELL MARCUS** when she gets back. She thinks he won't be able to tell. How can he separate the effects of yoga and sun from the effects of daily lovemaking?

But Marcus knows.

**JAY GOES BACK TO HIS APARTMENT** and looks around at his meagre belongings. The next day he buys a couch and a kitchen table and chairs. Leah won't know the difference.

But Leah can tell.

**IT SNOWS A COUPLE OF WEEKS AFTER THEY RETURN FROM MEXICO.** Everyone's talking about how strange it is, but Marcus reminds Leah that it usually gets cold in March, and often snows a little once the crocuses are out. She knows he remembers this because he stays inside when it snows; it's hard moving through it on wheels.

Leah still takes her walks but now, she does not go in disguise. Now, at least once a week, she arranges them around Jay's schedule. It is during this snowfall that they find themselves walking through a wooded section of Beacon Hill Park. Jay takes her hand as they walk, which is against their rules. If anyone they know sees them, their story is that he's an old friend from university. But today they are on their own. It is quiet and dark in the trees, and when Jay pulls her behind a big Douglas Fir they kiss like it's been months. It's only been a couple of days. They are hungry for each other; it seems like their plans have failed. They decide to cut the walk short and head to Jay's apartment, which is just around the corner from the park.

On the way, they pass through the snow-covered lawns, their tans looking orange in the pale light. All of a sudden, Jay stops and drops backwards onto the ground.

"What are you doing?" Leah asks.

He starts moving his arms and legs back and forth.

"Okay, there, kiddo," Leah says. "We don't have much time."

"I want you to do something for me," Jay says.

"What is it?"

He stops moving his limbs. "Stand at my feet, and help me out of here."

"Good thing we've been doing yoga," she says. She squats at his feet and extends her arms. He grabs on, and slowly, she leans back and Jay rolls his spine up out of the snow. Once he's sitting she pulls harder and instead of him pulling back, as they did in Mexico, to open their lower backs, he lets himself be pulled forward. Leah slips, and Jay falls on top of her, and they are a tangle of scarves and limbs and lips.

When they are on their feet again, they stand there, looking at his angel. The top looks good, untouched, but the bottom half is ruined, just a mess of footprints and grass from below the snow.

"I've never been able to get out of one of those without destroying it," Jay says.

"It's impossible. But it's still beautiful."

"My Buddhist practice this time around. Leaving a perfect imprint." Jay takes Leah's hand. "Shall we?"

Leah is still looking at the angel. She knows Marcus will never be able to do this again. But one day Jay will not be able to do this, either. Neither will she. One day this affair will be over and she will be in the same position she is in, loving a man who can't give her everything she needs. No one can give you everything. She knows there are no perfect angels; just ones made by humans, here on the earth they are bound to, for better or worse.

**A FEW WEEKS LATER, JAY JAMS HIS BACK AGAIN.** He takes the bus to work, because it hurts him to bike, and it is from the window of this bus as it waits at a red light, while an elderly man is coughing into his gloves behind him, while a child starts screaming because her mother won't let her push the stop button, it is then that he sees Leah on the sidewalk. He hasn't seen her since the walk in the snow. She won't call him; he can't call her. He doesn't know what happened. He sits on his new couch and waits, feeling his lower back shift out of place. He hasn't even called Ann. He wants to be available, in case Leah calls.

Leah is waiting for the light to change, with her hands in the pockets of her coat. Jay doesn't need to feel it to know that it is velvet. He can tell by the way the light strikes the cloth, becomes absorbed by it, then turns back around and demands to be seen again, strengthened, embodied. A solid column of fuchsia holds Leah as she waits for the hand on the traffic light to disappear so the walking man can let her cross. No wig; no glasses.

As the bus pulls through the intersection, Jay fumbles to push the button to get out at the next stop. The "stop requested" light is already on.

"Sorry, not this one," the mother of the screaming child calls to the driver. "She's faster than I am today." She yanks her daughter back onto her knee.

The stop requested light goes out. Jay watches Leah walk, her arms swinging now, full of intention, as if she has somewhere important to be.

He knocks on the window; he waves. She doesn't hear him. He fumbles for the button to make the light come on, then runs to the door as the bus speeds past her. It's another full block to the next stop. He watches as she gets lost among the other pedestrians, coming and going from town; as the bus drives away from her, he waits by the doors to get out.

**MARCUS AND TOBY ARE MAKING** a surprise dinner for Leah. With the list in his pocket, they go to the store while she's out walking. He fills his basket with the ingredients for Greek salad, which he plans to serve alongside spanakopita and rice. These are some of her favourite foods. He's been thinking about Leah in these terms lately: what makes her hum, what doesn't. Last week, while she was massaging his shoulders, she hinted at what happened in Mexico. "It's not what I wanted," she said, pressing her cheek against his. "It made me miss you too much."

Marcus didn't ask for details. He didn't know if he wanted them or not. He tried to imagine if things were reversed, if he were the one being asked to break the rules, and whether he would want to tell her about it. He wouldn't.

If only he could trade places with her. Because sometimes, he believes that she has lost more than he has. He would take the divide between able-bodied and messed-up, and make it his to bridge. Make the uncertainty of her future, his. He knows what his future holds, what the limitations will be. His losses have already been grieved over. Every time Leah looks at him, he knows she sees what she's lost. Every time he looks at her, he is reminded of what he still has.

He and Toby worked out a kind of rhythm while Leah was away, and they fall back into it easily as they make this meal for her. They have it timed out: they know to wait until Leah is home to start the rice and warm up the spanakopita. The salad can be made now, so the flavours mix. Toby measures the dressing ingredients into a jar and shakes it before pouring the dressing over the vegetables and feta cheese.

While they wait for her to return, they play a snowboarding video game. They have it turned down low, so they can hear her footsteps as she approaches the house. Marcus wants to have the game off and the oven on by the time she is in the kitchen. Everything is set: all they need is Leah, to come home and tell them about what she's seen, out there, on one of the first real spring afternoons.

# APPROPRIATE

**ANDRA IS TANNING ON HER SUNDECK.** She's been here for ten minutes, and she's going to wait another ten before opening her tube of sunscreen. Donnie Donaldson, the downstairs tenant's little boy, is digging in the garden below her. Donnie Donaldson. Something no child should have to be called. No one has checked on him in half an hour. Andra watches him furiously scrubbing away at a patch of dirt, his small hands flying. She wonders if he's trying to get to China, or if kids even bother to do that anymore.

Once, she gave birth to a child, no bigger than a rainbow trout. It was alive when she pushed it into the world, and dead within an hour. All of its parts were there—it was nearly six months old—but it wasn't big enough to survive outside of her. Its appendages had moved against the walls of her abdomen like fins.

Donnie is digging for something. The treasure! he exclaims. I must find the treasure! Andra planted seeds there, last summer, sweet peas she soaked in water for two days before planting, but nothing came up. She is tempted to get up from her chair and call down to him. Hey, what are you doing? She has asked him not to mess about with her garden, and in the spring, when he was shovelling soil into a pail of water, he told her it was potion. I've added ground-up chalk, he said. She could see the footprints from his magic for days afterwards on the sidewalk, muddy trails of frantic chase. Today she doesn't want to be the upstairs ogre, always watching out for mess or danger. She just wants to infuse herself with sun.

Yesterday, Andra heard from Jay. He is a poet. He is also her ex-boyfriend, and the man who fathered the baby. They haven't spoken in a year, not since the day he moved out after telling her he was tired of her cheerfulness. You're too happy, he told her. Why can't you just feel it? Feel what? she asked. Life, he said. It's not always okay. They had birthed the child at home, in the bathroom, because it had come without warning.

Eventually, they wrapped it in a face cloth, then a sheet of Japanese paper, so it looked like a gift, not a dead body. Jay wanted to take it to the end of the breakwater, and drop it in, out where the oystercatchers fished. She was horrified. There was no way she could let the ocean have it. The earth was foreign, too, but at least she could visit the burial place and know the baby's bones were beneath her. They buried the baby in Andra's family plot, and gave it a headstone carved with a small fish. What did she say? She can't remember. She was leaning on her mother's shoulder, breasts aching with milk. But she remembers what he said, through his tears: it wasn't meant to be.

**EVERY DAY, ANDRA HEARS** Mr. Donaldson and his son talking and moving around in the apartment below. She walks into her kitchen and hears Donnie playing a computer game, shouting and calling out "Awesome!" She goes down her dark hallway and lies on her bed and listens to Mr. Donaldson and his girlfriend doing it, sometimes with the addition of porn. She hears the theatrical moaning of the movie, the wockachicka-wockachicka of the bad music, the build to the inevitable release. She wonders if her footsteps above them are a distraction, or if they give her any thought at all, making the noises they make. It makes her crazy, all this knowledge of their private lives, the names and crutches they need to use to get off.

From below she hears other, more normal sounds as well. The toilet flushing, because it makes the water in her toilet run for a couple of seconds. Mr. Donaldson's cell phone, set to play the 1812 overture. The raucous play of five year olds yelling Charge! and To the Dungeon. The long, low wail of the boy when he's overtired and has to go to bed. The bath water being run, and once, the father's car right after. She opened her curtain to watch him leave, alone. She watched the clock: a person can drown in two inches of water. Five minutes and they're beyond resuscitation. He came back ten minutes later, a Starbucks cup in one hand, cell in the other (she was keeping watch from behind the blinds). She heard him call out to the boy. Donnie, you okay? No reply. Donnie? A rattle of the locked bathroom door handle. Donnie? She waited above them in her own bathroom for what seemed like forever, until she heard him faintly answer. I'm all right.

When she found out she was expecting, she didn't believe it. Of course, she herself had been an unplanned baby, but now things were so much easier. Why had she let it slide? She and Jay weren't even living together at the time. The label "my boyfriend" suddenly became "my partner." As if the idea to grow a baby was decided upon, in the partnership. A business decision, made over a couple of drinks.

After she got over the initial shock, she was amazed at how she had become the ultimate marketing target. The magazine covers, the advertisements: so many were now aimed directly at her, First Time Mom, ready to be shaped by media and tradition into a woman who loses herself in the quest for the perfect child.

THE JEALOUSY BONE

She didn't care one way or the other about the family bed or pacifiers or rocking chairs. But Jay was so happy, ecstatic even, that she couldn't bring herself to tell him of her ambivalence. If he knew, and he probably did, he overcompensated for it by carrying the bulk of the joy for the first three months, until the sickness subsided. Only when Andra felt the baby kicking inside her, did she allow herself to believe that she could do this, carry a child and bring it forth. She would worry about the parenting afterwards. For the time being, she was an aquarium, holding a being meant for another place.

"How long did you push?" and "Did you tell you partner you hated him, like I did?" were questions she was never asked. When the baby was gone, she just looked bigger, rolls spilling out over her waistband with average-sized hips and legs below. Without a sling or Snugli or 3-in-1 stroller, she was just another woman carrying her weight around the middle. Although it was something that made her laugh now, she had even thought of carrying a doll with her, slung across her torso. But she knew people would expect to be able to touch the baby's cheek, examine its face for resemblance, feed their fingers into its fist to feel the grip.

**JAY DIDN'T SAY HELLO** when she picked up the phone. Only her name, in that heavy voice of his, as if he had to add weight to whatever he was saying. "Andra."

She had imagined this moment, had tossed around phrases for nearly a year, building her words into tools she could use against him. But all she said was, "Yes. Hello."

"I need to see you."

The soap opera line coming from him, in that tone, was actually beguiling. It had been so long since she'd felt the vibration of that voice, or any man's voice, so close to her ear, she wasn't sure she had the strength to fight it. She took a deep breath.

"I have to talk to you about something, Andra."

Either he was in trouble or she was. Her mind leapt to HIV, other STDs, maxed credit cards in her name. Marriage, maybe. Was he in love with someone, already? "Okay," she said. "I'm listening."

"No," he said. "It's not appropriate for the telephone."

God. Even he was using the latest term she'd heard too often at the park during lunch hour. "Sammy, it's not appropriate to eat sand." "Mugs, it's not appropriate to chew on a stranger's leg." "That's inappropriate, Ashley, Mommy doesn't like being kicked in the shins." Leaving your son in the bathtub while you go for coffee is not appropriate, Mr. Donaldson, she wanted to say to her neighbour whenever she saw him. Maybe the latest jargon would get through to him. But she always just gave him a cool nod: let him figure it out.

"Are you in town?"

"Yes." He sounded relieved. "Meet me at the coffee shop in half an hour? The one we used to go to, on Seventh."

"Fine," she said. Curiosity had gotten her. "I'll be the one in black."

This had been a joke of theirs. Counting the number of people drinking specialty coffees who were wearing only black. The numbers escalated easily. It was something they did every time they went to that coffee shop. Andra never wore black. It made her pale skin look plastic and overworked.

He didn't laugh. She hung up the phone and pulled herself together.

**ANDRA HAD FOUND A PHOTOGRAPH** a month after Jay moved out, behind the shelf paper in the medicine cabinet. He would describe the photograph as a piece of art. His brother had died a year before the baby, and he had taken a picture of him, in his casket. Then he photoshopped a picture of the baby, lying in the foetal position, into his brother's hands. Andra found it right about the time that she was learning to dream of other things than going fishing and pulling up rotten salmon with missing eyes; Jay had made a strong case for the ocean burial, and in her dreams she was sometimes convinced that the baby was in the sea. She put the photo back where she found it and resolved not to look at it again.

**AT THE COFFEE SHOP** she took a seat at the window, on one of the high stools. They were the least comfortable chairs in the place, but she wanted a view to distract her.

"Andra." Jay put his hand on her upper arm.

She looked into Jay's face. She waited for him to comment on her freshly streaked hair, her newly emerged body, her glasses-free eyes. But all he said was, "You're not wearing black."

"It was all in the wash." She smiled against her will.

He sat down on the stool beside her and set his coffee cup on the table. They stared out the window for a minute, both with their hands wrapped tightly around their mugs, and watched the sparrows foraging around the metal tables.

"The way we left things—"

"It wasn't meant to be." Andra kept her eyes on the birds.

"You sound pretty sure about that."

She whipped her head around to stare at him. "Jay, that's what you said. About the baby."

"I was in a bad state. I didn't mean it."

"Right."

"I didn't know what I was saying. I was mourning."

"That's funny," she said. "So was I." Her hands smoothed her hair back into submission. Even using three different hair products was not enough to subdue its frizzled mass.

"I'm sorry."

She picked up a newspaper and opened it to the comics.

"Andra—I left something in your apartment."

She looked at him again. His skin looked tanned. His eyes seemed a lighter grey than they were before. He was wearing a woven cotton shirt, either Mexican or Guatemalan. "You left a lot of things. I put them at the curb months ago."

"You wouldn't have thrown this out."

"It's not there anymore." She started reading the paper again. Should she play with him a little? She glanced at her watch. "You're talking about the photograph."

"You didn't, Andra. Please tell me you didn't throw it out."

"Why would I keep it? Do you think I need that kind of thing hanging around my apartment?"

"You had no right to throw it away. It was mine." He took the paper out of her hands.

"It gave me the creeps," she said, reaching for the paper. "And if you don't mind—"

"You can't look at your own baby? Are you still trying to pretend that it didn't happen?"

Andra picked at the pills on the sleeve of her sweater. "I'm trying to move on," she said quietly.

Jay looked at her until she looked back at him. "Is it that hard to look at me? Are you really that angry?"

"What do you want the photo for, anyway?" she asked. "Do you have another use for it now? Another way to feed your 'artists' soul'?"

"No." His shoulders sagged. "I just want to see it again."

Andra slid off the stool and started winding her long green and blue striped scarf around her neck. She only reached his shoulder

THE JEALOUSY BONE

when she was standing on the floor. "Listen," she said, "I've gotta work at noon."

Jay waited. He stirred his cold coffee.

"Well?" she said. "Are you coming or not?"

**DONNIE WAS PLAYING ON THE STEPS** when they arrived at the house. Donnie and Jay were friends from the first day he moved in, back when Donnie was in preschool, still carrying Hot Wheels in both small fists wherever he went. After high fives all around, Jay pulled a quarter from behind Donnie's knee.

"Do that again!" Donnie cried. "I gotta get my Dad to see this."

"Donnie," Andra said. "We don't have time right now."

"I'll teach you how the next time, okay?" Jay said.

Andra shot him a look.

Donnie jumped up to give Jay another high five. "Okay!" he shouted. "You're awesome."

Jay followed Andra up the steep staircase. Once upon a time, he used to nip at her calves when they walked up together, barking like a terrier, making her squeal. Now they were both quiet, their eyes on every step.

Andra opened the door to her apartment and gestured for Jay to enter. "It's where you left it," she said. "I didn't know where else to put it."

Jay found the photo in the bathroom and brought it out to the living room. Two months into their relationship, his brother had killed himself. Jay had had to go to Montreal to identify the body, and clean up the drugs and what they had done to him. The note didn't mention gay, or AIDS, but he'd had to tell his parents this as well. He became the only son. The only child. He didn't write poetry for months. He would come to her apartment in the middle of the night and work out his grief in her, sob after coming, then telling her about the hours he had spent walking the empty city, looking for inspiration that didn't come. In the morning, he would be gone. It was a good day if she went into the bathroom and saw his footprints on the bathmat, wet imprints of his soles on the pale blue terrycloth. He was showering. Even though she liked the scent of him when he didn't shower—he smelled like a warm rock, lichen drying in the sun, like cat fur after a nap on the porch—at least if she saw those prints, she knew he had enough hope to keep himself clean.

Now, he walked around the room, slowly, holding the picture in one hand, idly picking up her books and photographs with the other. Andra went in the kitchen to pack herself a lunch.

"I wonder," Jay called, "if they know each other."

She knew he was talking about the baby and his brother. "What? Like in heaven?" she asked from inside the fridge, where she was looking for the alfalfa sprouts.

"Sure," Jay said, coming into the kitchen. "Why not?"

"It just seems so hokey," she said, although she had thought the same thing, many times. An uncle for her baby. Someone to watch out for her little one.

She washed some limp lettuce, then wrapped it in a tea towel and shook it with a flick of her wrist. Water sprayed over the dirty dishes in the sink.

Jay placed his hands on her shoulders. "Will you stop for a minute?"

She tried to shrug him off.

"I'm worried about you, Andra. I don't think you've grieved yet."

She looked into his eyes, grey and earnest, peering out at her from under his sun-bleached eyebrows. "Jay, you've got your picture. Why don't you go back to whatever exotic land you came from, and let me finish making my freaking lunch?"

He looked down at the photo. "This isn't why I came here." He gave a slight laugh. "You know me, I've got all of this on disc." He thrust the photo in front of her face.

Andra could only stare at it. Jay's brother inside his white coffin, the mollusc of her baby's body seeming to rest in his hands. She had forgotten how small it was. At the time, all they could think about was how close it had been to making it, nearly big enough to stay on this side of things, how close her body had been to making this child come to life.

He sat down at the table. "We would have made great parents. You know that, don't you?" He was smiling, a glow coming into his eyes: tears.

Andra started in on the sandwich again, spreading mayo on both pieces of bread. "I'm not even going there."

"You know it's true. It wasn't a mistake, us getting pregnant."

"A reason for everything. Right. Well, I don't buy that anymore."

"But we could try again, Andy. We could give it another shot."

They could hear someone thumping up the stairs. "Right on cue," Andra said. "That kid's all over you."

Andra reached the door before Donnie started knocking. She could see little E's of mud on every step, like a trail of cookies to help him find his way back. "Jay," Andra called. "Someone needs you over here."

He got up slowly from the table and met her on her way back to the kitchen. He stopped her with a hand on her arm. "All I'm asking is that you think about it." At the door, he crouched down until he was at eye level with Donnie and his pail full of dirty water. "Let me see your potion," he said. "What kind of magic do you want it to make?"

**THE FISH HAD BEEN A BABY,** and the baby had been a girl. If she had lived, she would be almost walking by now, ready to play peek-a-boo with her father. And despite her desire to think otherwise, she knew Jay would make a good father. He would know how to pull gold coins from behind her ponytail. He would let her move soil around in the backyard as much as she liked. He would let her draw horses with ten legs under a green sky if she wanted to. He would treat her like a gift, and hold her in his warm, soft hands.

After the boy was gone, Jay came back to wash his hands at the kitchen sink. "Look around you," he said, gesturing to the apartment. "This huge empty space. And no one to fill it."

"You don't know me anymore," she said. "I have everything I need."

ANDRA SQUEEZES SUNSCREEN INTO HER PALM, then rubs her hands together and smears her face and arms with it. Donnie is still digging in her garden.

Jay has phoned her five times since yesterday, leaving messages on her machine about destiny and fate. What he doesn't know is that she has thought of having another child many times since the first one died. Of course she has; it's a natural response. But she doesn't want to test herself like this. If she's defective, she's not ready to know.

When Donnie feels her staring at him, he looks up and gives her a little wave. She might go down and join him. She wants to be there if he finds his treasure. If he finds it, she knows it will be something ordinary, transformed into treasure beneath the ordinary earth. She will take her sunscreen to him. Even from a height, she can see that the back of his neck has already turned a dangerous shade of pink.

# ANTIDOTE

**DREW AND APRIL** sat across from each other at the Red Mango Café. It was two weeks after April had left, telling Drew only that she needed some time to herself. This was not unusual. She had always been the type to get away. She liked to have space around her and uninterrupted light coming in the windows for her paintings— watercolours that were finally beginning to sell. Last year she had rented a seaside cabin for ten days, hauled water, fought off mice in order to have this light. But it wasn't temporary this time: April wanted out of the marriage.

Drew rested his forehead against his palm, thumb and ring finger on his temples, stretching the skin just enough to feel it burn. From this position he watched his pulse jump. In his wrist were many bits of anatomy he could not name, or see, or muster enough curiosity to care about, but this jumping artery reminded him that his body was doing things without his consent. That his heart still managed to keep its rhythm, in the face of April's news, was either a sign of mutiny or a sign of loyalty. He couldn't decide.

He looked at his wife, who was strumming her cheek and staring out the window at the rooftops and sky. April had a habit, too, of flicking the muscles under her cheekbones with her thumb, when her head rested against her fingertips. It made her streaked bangs bounce, just a little (bangs, at her age!). Someday she was going to loosen those muscles enough for them to come out, scooped like clams from their shells.

Drew had some questions today. To start with, what kind of woman tells you she's leaving you, over an early lunch, in a café you had brunched in for years after making weekend love? What kind of woman wears her silky red blouse to this outing, the one that plunges and ripples with only a breath across the table? What kind of woman, and this is the biggest question of all for Drew, what kind of woman—a real artist for God's sakes—falls for a housepainter? In all his life, he'd never met such a woman, and now he was married to one, had been married to one for a number of years, apparently, who was sitting across from him, lost in thought.

A blush had appeared in her cheeks that didn't correspond to the area of thumb prying but must be, Drew realized, from the thought of screwing this housepainter, a man Drew had seen many times in the past few weeks through the picture window, hanging off a ladder at his own house, his blue-splattered runners perilously close to slipping off the rungs. For hours he had watched this man going up and down the ladder with paint cans full of that blue, a shade Drew's wife had chosen because it matched the flowers she grew in teapots all along the railing of the porch.

April had wanted to brighten up the place. New energy. Attract an abundance of creativity with the fresh new look, and other forms of horseshit. Her night table used to be stacked with library books on creating a new reality. Now Drew was afraid he was going to have to give some credit to all that nonsense. How else would April have found this painter-boy, if not by manifesting him out of thin, incense-laden air?

A revelation came to Drew: she would take the teapots with her. And then he would be alone in a baby blue house. The thought of it made him queasy.

## DREW, SHE SAID. YOU'RE SWEATING.

He was. He looked down at his plate, still loaded with mixed greens and raspberry vinaigrette. A half-eaten piece of foccacia teetered on the edge of the plate. Nothing he could blame the sweating on. But why shouldn't he be sweating? His whole life was broken now. He was holding it together quite well, as far as he was concerned.

A touch of the flu, he said, then took a huge gulp of water. The college is rampant with it. He taught in a broadcast and communications program. At the moment, he couldn't remember his schedule past the afternoon, when he was supposed to talk about vocal development for radio. He would call in sick. He would let the kids have a free afternoon, so he could go home and recover. But how do you recover from something like this? What could he tell admin about his prognosis?

April had eaten most of her grilled panini. Now, suddenly, she suddenly started rummaging through her purse. Probably in search of gum. She was trying too hard. She'd always hated gum, yet he'd seen her with a wad of the stuff a few times over the past month. They should both be well beyond the gum chewing stage; they had no business chewing gum at all. Gum was for children, for smart-alecks, for ex-smokers—but no, she wasn't looking for gum. April had pulled out a miniscule plastic vial and was now thrusting it into Drew's face.

Here. This is the best thing for it.

For what? Drew pulled his head back like a turtle and looked through the bottom of his bifocals. What is it?

Homeopathic. If you catch it in time, the flu will be gone tonight.

Drew gave a half-snort, half-laugh. I highly doubt it.

Give it a try. It's not going to kill you.

But I'm not sick, he wanted to shout. I've just been told my wife is leaving me, is all, honey. Do you have any potions for that in your bag of tricks?

Drew opened his hand and April set the white tube into his palm. Take the whole thing at once. And no coffee or mint or eating for half an hour.

He shook his head. Ridiculous. He tried to pry the lid off with his fingers, but suddenly he felt weak, as if the flu was in that bottle, making his limbs turn to Jell-o. Wasn't it *like* curing *like*? Wouldn't he get sick if he wasn't already? Maybe he shouldn't take it. Drew hardly ever took sick days. He was entitled to feeling ill right about now. But wait a minute. He wasn't sick. Was he?

Just pull it off with your teeth, April said. Here, let me show you.

I can do it. He bit the soft plastic top off. Inside were hundreds of round white balls the size of pinheads. He felt like he was on Candid Camera, or something like that, like April was pulling something insane on him as a parting gift. These weren't really medicinal, they were really made of something space-aged that would expand upon contact with his saliva and render him speechless while she told him all about the fucking love of her life.

Pour the whole thing into your mouth, she said, then let them dissolve. They taste good. They're lactose.

He emptied the vial onto his tongue. They felt like a mouthful of poppy seeds. He rolled them against the roof of his mouth and they hurt him a little. That alone made him feel a tiny bit better. Maybe they weren't a ploy. Maybe this wasn't as crazy as it seemed.

You'll feel better soon, she said, and picked up her latté.

Drew stared at her.

What is it?

You could've at least talked to me at home, he said, trying to tuck the medicine under his tongue. This place—this isn't where I want to be for this. He could feel a few balls collecting in the corners of his mouth, threatening to spill out. He could feel tears gathering too. It had been years since he'd cried. Years.

I know, April said. I'm sorry. But, well... he's there right now, finishing up the trim. I didn't want it to be awkward. She started stacking creamers in front of her plate.

Sorry? Awkward? You don't find the whole situation a little awkward?

Well, yes, it is a little surprising... She was studying the creamers now, adjusting the gaps, making it look like a sculpture, something someone would pay for.

April. This is more than that. Drew pushed his plate towards her and made the creamers topple. They sat, in silence, April looking out the window again, as if she had never seen that skyline before, while Drew let the granules slowly dissolve into a sweet nothingness.

Do you know what you've done? Drew asked her quietly. He wiped fiercely at his face, circling his eyes to get rid of the evidence. Have you thought about any of this?

April didn't look at him. I've given it plenty of thought.

It sounded like she had made a choice. Drew couldn't get past this. It wasn't like he was April's doctor, or colleague, someone she might've built up a connection with, over time. This would make sense, if Drew had to make sense of it. But a painter? She hardly knew him: three weeks at the most. Wasn't that when they'd hired the man?

If only the world were black and white. Then, instead of having chosen a housepainter with which to make glorious animal love, April might be back at the house, talking to him about how both of them could put more effort into the marriage. He knew she had her art and her job at the gallery; he didn't expect her undivided attention. When he got home, they would talk about the CBC strike, the lack of anything good on the airwaves, the state of the next generation, the lack of respect in his students, their sense of entitlement. She would be there, on his side, agreeing with his opinions, asking for them.

But the world was not black and white. Instead they had chosen a ridiculous shade of blue for the siding, and April was hiring movers to pick up her share of things in a week.

DREW FINALLY CRACKED the carapace of silence around their table. What's his name?

April jerked her eyes away from the view. Who, Sammy's?

Sammy? Drew said this too loudly. The women at the next table contracted their eyebrows. *Sammy?*

I can't believe you didn't even know his name, April said. He's been around our house for a month.

Obviously, I haven't been. He raised his cup of coffee to his mouth.

Don't! April cried. You'll ruin the medicine.

Drew put his cup down. Oh, this was precious. His wife was fussing about a little sip of java, afraid for him that he would not get rid of the flu. As if she *cared* about him, as if she wanted what was *best* for him, sitting across from him in her sexy red blouse meant for another man. As if he was still so controlled by this woman who had no control of her own, as if he would maintain this charade he'd begun by claiming influenza in the first place.

And yet he reached for his water glass and took a swig from that instead.

April stood and excused herself. Little girls' room, she said.

It was the first time she'd ever said that to Drew. She was turning cute. She pulled at her blouse to minimize the cleavage—as if Drew had never seen what was beneath it. He watched her purse, hugging

her left hip, the strap slung across her back and of course simultane-
ously across her chest, where he had laid his head, listening to her
syncopations, thinking of her heart as an opening, a closing shell.

The waiters smiled at her. Drew knew she was smiling back. He
knew she was going to freshen her lipstick in the bathroom. He knew
*Sammy* would like his women dolled up like masked avengers. Where
Drew picked that particular phrase, he wasn't sure, but he liked it. He
took a sip of his coffee, medicine be damned. The cream had left an
oily residue on top, a slick of cow fat laminating his tongue.

I will get through today, and tonight, and tomorrow, he told himself, head in hands. After all is said and done, when have you not been
okay? This was a line he'd heard someone say on the subway, a mother
talking to her daughter about money. The universe looks after you,
the mother said. Drew had no idea what he would have told the girl,
who had been fired from her job at a bookstore.

There had been no children for April and Drew. Not as messy,
friends would be saying; be thankful for that. But thankful was a
foreign concept at the moment. Thankful was on a ship sailing rapidly
south for a sunny holiday. Thankful was entirely wrong.

A housepainter. What was worst of all was that she, an *actual*
painter, referred to him as one as well. He imagined this kid going
to parties where he, Drew, should be, but isn't, telling people he's a
painter. I'm a painter, he'd say, and they'd say, Oh, another artist, eh?
What sort of paintings? they would ask, thinking they might recognize
the work, or perhaps want to buy something down the road.

It was one of those things about the language that drove him
mad. He was a small / medium / large man in a tall / grande / venti
world. Partner did not mean wife. Wife meant you were a farmer in
the dell, taking her, and she the child, and the child the dog, and so
on, right up until you had the cheese, standing alone. The farmer
was not alone.

Drew's stomach was rolling thunderously. Often this happened
before he stood in front of his class, about to deliver the lecture on

sex in the media. All those ultra-cool students tittering at an old man using the word *genitals*. His stomach had done this on their wedding day, too, not even stopping once the two of them were alone and April rested her tired head on his belly. Now, though, looking at his uneaten salad, he merely put it down to hunger. Another example of his body's mutinous ways, and after those damned mini balls, he couldn't eat for another twenty minutes. He reached over to the empty table next to them and grabbed their creamers, adding to the fallen artwork his wife had begun. A co-creation, coming a little too late... He placed his creamers strategically, to try and block himself from seeing her fingers when she returned. Already, the ring for which he'd sold his first car was gone.

He could've dealt with someone else, given time. God knows their relationship had seen stronger days, or years. A separation of interests, a natural movement towards members of their own sexes, hobby-wise, that was par for the course. A painter, though. A G.D. house painter. Doesn't she know the fumes will make him crazy, if they haven't already?

That's my problem, he realized. I'm not crazy enough. I wear too much brown and tan. I don't have holes in my t-shirts, or, if I do, I throw them in the rag drawer. I eat two pieces of toast every morning, jam on one and peanut butter on the other, and I probably will continue to do so for the rest of my life. When we went to Mexico, I paid nearly eight dollars for it. I even learned how to say *crema de cacahuate* because I couldn't sway from the pattern.

He wanted to shout at April: it's called reliability! But he couldn't shout, not in a restaurant, which was precisely her motive in bringing him here. He couldn't shout anyway, not in the state he was in.

April was back from the bathroom. She had just finished her cup of coffee, which wasn't fair, and she was looking at him, expectantly.

Drew, she said.

She wanted a reaction. His wife wanted him to say something. She'd put in her time with him, across tables like this. She wanted

THE JEALOUSY BONE

fireworks, or waterworks, maybe. He knew she was searching his face for something she could call emotion—the thing she'd always wanted more of—but he had wiped the traces away.

Maybe he should try shouting anyway. Maybe this was his last chance. His one more chance. If he got it right, he'd win the prize. If he blew up from grief or anger or jealousy or love, she'd take him back. Drew looked into her expectant eyes. Her eyelashes seemed longer—or, curlier. Yes, they were definitely curled. How does one curl eyelashes, he wondered. A pen? Some kind of heated device? And, why did she do this? For whom?

He would say something horrible. He would work it into some sort of monster he could spring upon her, unleash in her prettied-up face.

Drew?

Or he would cry—not a stretch today—and tell her of his own slip-up, something he could cook up in a few seconds, lightly embellish as he went along, giving her this in exchange for hers. A student, maybe, something so stereotypical she couldn't doubt him, or hold it against him, completely. Then they would call it even. They would refer to it only once or twice in the course of their marriage from this point in, from this checkpoint. The race wasn't over. This was just a stop for electrolytes.

Yes, she would tell him she'd gone mad. She would see his heart on the table like a dessert they would share, and he would feel his stomach settle, and then they would help each other into their coats, like the old people they were about to become, this nasty blip in their relationship a kind of milestone, and then they would go home.

But when he opened his mouth, his words were granular. They meant nothing. Little words for which the antidote could be practically anything at all.

# THE JEALOUSY BONE

**WE START OUR AFTER-DINNER TOUR** on the bottom floor. Three flamingos stretch the spaces, stripes of coral, dashes of black for bills. The token toucan, its bill tucked alongside a wing, is asleep; all the other birds in Crystal Gardens can hide their whole beaks in their feathers, but the toucan can only approximate. Five pygmy marmosets chase each other around a bedraggled hanging fern, their miniature faces like rubber stamps of sadness.

"It's not fair." I'm talking about the whole setup. You tell me we couldn't see these animals without this kind of place. Do they want to be seen? The ring-tailed lemurs are flinging themselves around their enclosures like fed-up teenagers, staring out at us with gold-rimmed eyes.

We walk the jungled pathways. We feel the spray from the artificial waterfall. We watch koi the size of salmon sleeping in their few inches of water. You toast your boss with your glass of ginger ale and applaud his choice of the Gardens for the Christmas party this year. We kiss on the bridge.

"I feel funny," I say. "There are too many eyes in here."

"Relax," you say. "Birds do it, bees do it."

"Is everything a flipping song to you?"

"Yes," you say, trying to kiss my neck.

I duck under your arm. "I gotta go," I say. "Call of nature."

The bathroom stalls are the colour of melted creamsicles. A woman with tinsel criss-crossing her torso says, "I look ridiculous. I thought people were going to dress up." The air is gelatinous with perfume. I swipe a look at myself, twist my skirt back to centre alignment, stick my fingers in my hair like it's grass and pull upwards. Bite my lips to bring out their best.

When I come out, a DJ's playing generation-spanning songs, The Beatles to ABBA, Van Halen to Madonna. A woman in a gold velour skirt is twirling her hips and two men are watching her as her arms escalate and a sliver of a breast appears on either side of her halter top. She leaves with both of them, down to the monkey display. Then, from the top of the stairs, I see them going farther, into the room where the fruit bats fold and unfold their wings as they eat suspended pears and melons. The black-out simulating nightfall, fooling them into flight. Ten minutes later she emerges with one of the men, tugging her top until the seams run straight. You still haven't found me. I browse the dessert table again, lift the silver lid from the triangles of Christmas pudding for the second time, just to smell the rum sauce. The other man comes whistling up the stairs. I order a special coffee. Dip a stale shortbread in and suck.

"Sorry I took so long," you say, with a walk that makes your tie swing like a tail. I cautioned you against the thing but it was a point you had to make: I can tie my own necktie. You're the only man under fifty wearing one. At least yours doesn't have Bart Simpson on it, wearing a wreath around his neck. "The boss cornered me in the loo."

"Sounds scary," I say. "What time does the band go on?"

"Let me go ask." And – poof – Mr. Front Desk Manager, Mr. Service Provider, you're gone again.

**THIS CITY IS GETTING TOO DAMN SMALL.** I haven't told you this, but I know the drummer of the band that's coming on soon. He took me out for a drink before I met you, only weeks before, in fact, but then his grandmother got sick and he left town for awhile. Things might've progressed. You want to be a musician too: you're forever hammering out rhythms on the dryer, the steering wheel, singing into ice cream cones. I've tried to get you to take lessons but you tell me you don't have the time. What pressing engagements—*Law & Order* reruns aside—are crowding your calendar? Now Jacko is playing at your Christmas party, playing so we can dance in the refracted light with your co-workers and call it a night to remember.

You bustle back. "Should be up there in ten."

"Then we have time for the butterflies." I steer you toward the glass enclosure. Inside the butterfly room I watch as insects land on your blue shirt. We spend ten minutes inside and the broad-winged azure butterfly stays on your chest the whole time. While we hunt for others in the orchids, I imagine how one would feel on my skin, the miniscule movements of its wings, the tiniest of eyelash kisses. I stick my forearm into the face of every butterfly we see, but none finds me appealing. I come up close to you, hoping you'll hand yours off like an infant to an aunt. But you just look at me with that beatific smile, and the butterfly, camouflaged on poly-cotton, doesn't move.

"They're attracted to salt," you tell me. "Wanna get sweaty?"

You mean dancing.

**BACK ON THE DANCE FLOOR,** I can see your shoulder blades through your shirt after five minutes. My hair is wilting in the humid air. We're in monsoon season, in the Great Canadian Indoors. Something we have to pay for here, something we can leave after the party's over.

"Having fun?" you ask. The band still hasn't finished setting up.

I give you the see-saw yes. A head wobble. Non-committal.

You point to the stage with your virgin hitchhiker thumb. "Hope they're good."

What if they're not? "I'll be right back," I say. My skirt has done the twist along with me, and I can't get it right without a mirror. "Bathroom again."

A concerned look crosses your face. "Not another bladder...?"

I shake my head as I'm walking away. Rearrange my face into a smile, which is still there when Jacko spots me from across the room. I pretend not to see him.

**THIS IS OUR FIRST CHRISTMAS.** We were an early spring set-up that's lasted three seasons. At the beginning, you told me, "I don't have a jealous bone in my body." We were sitting on a bench in the park, watching people bloat the ducks' bellies with white buns. "You don't need to worry about that, at least." Like I had asked you for your genetic makeup, or an STD test. Sign here if you're going to hurt someone for looking at me. As if I'd be relieved.

**IT SEEMS JACKO HAS COME AROUND THE OTHER WAY,** so that I run into him outside the bathrooms, in front of the flamingos. My skirt is still askew.

"You're back in town," I say. "How's your grandmother?'

"Dead. I was only away for three weeks."

My cheeks heat up. "I'm sorry." I can hear the rest of the band tuning up.

"You work for these guys?"

"No," I say. "I'm just here for the party."

"Right." His eyes are on my crooked seam, following the front of my left thigh down to my calf. "So what's new?"

I laugh, breezily. "Oh, not much. The usual work, sleep, eat kind of thing."

His eyes are rising above the waist now. "Well, don't let me keep you." He points at the bathroom door.

"Oh. Yeah. Well. Actually, I was just going to check out the butterflies. I hear they're amazing."

"I've never seen them," he says. "Mind if I tag along?"

You wouldn't mind, right? It's just to see some butterflies.

**AFTER A SATISFACTORY SUMMER** of weekend trips to the lakes, things got busy. We weren't seeing enough of each other, you said, with your schedule and my habit of sleeping in, so we took a trip. An autumn special to Edmonton. The whisper in my ear promised me hotel robes, a shower that didn't go cold before the conditioner set, clearance racks at their absurdity of a mall. All of it enticed me, but none of it was enough. Then I caught a whiff of your matching Paco Rabanne deodorant and aftershave, and it buoyed me up. The complexity of chemicals against your warm, animal flesh. The safe excitement in that enveloping waft as you reached into your wallet to get your MasterCard.

I started breathing through my turtleneck just after we reached our cruising altitude, to warm myself up. You didn't like it. You said you needed to see my chin. My eyes were not enough. You might've mistaken me for someone else, someone dangerous, maybe, sitting in the aisle seat, ready to do something to take the airplane down. But dammit, it was cold in there. And I needed the scent of cotton, and farther down, the scent of my own skin, to get relief. All of that air pulled through the nostrils of everyone else, like we were all one monster with two hundred swivelling heads: instant influenza. The whole thing smelled like a used Kleenex. I wondered if this would be worth a disease.

"Please," you said, taking a deep breath, oblivious to what you were inviting in. "Cut it out".

"It's called nagging," I said, through the fabric, "when you say it twice."

As I'm on my way back to the dance floor, I realize, after so many bathroom visits, you might jump to the conclusion that I'm pregnant. Not that it would be an easy leap for anyone else, but you've been looking at babies lately now that all the office women are having them and bringing them in to pass around. You're getting awfully good at shopping for lullaby CDs and undershirts; you've been talking like a demented mathematician, working out probabilities of eye colour if we were ever to conceive such a thing. I bet you've thought it all through by the time I get back. You want me to have a home birth, name it after your father, throw it in the pool at six months to watch instinct kick in. Sink or swim. That damned grin on your face when I return, like you're about to hand out blue-ribboned cigars.

"I just had to fix my skirt," I say. It's partly true. "What are you so happy for?"

The band starts with "Every Breath you Take," to ease us into the mood.

"This is about obsession," I say into your ear as we're dancing slow.

You squeeze my waist, smiling. "You think too much. Just enjoy the song."

I don't tell you that thinking is something I can't control. I never promised you a Zen garden. Your fingers on the skin between skirt and top, feeling for extra pudge as evidence. You can stop doing that at any time. I press this into a thought bullet and shoot right into your ear. But you don't stop.

This is the test for jealousy bones: no x-rays necessary. We're dancing up close to the stage. I'm leaning forward with certain beats, letting my spaghetti straps slide off my shoulders. Jacko is watching me, his eyes meeting mine every eighth beat. You haven't noticed. The smile on your face is the same one you came in with, the same one you'll leave with. It goes with the tie and dress pants: those muscles have contracted and held, a spasm no one knows how to release.

Jacko isn't smiling. He's got the face of a gargoyle, perched on his stool, hitting the cymbals like they've let him down. His simian hair covers his eyes with every head thrust. But I can see him just fine.

Unlike anyone around us, you actually dance as if no one's watching: you've taken that magnet message from our fridge into your heart and it's gone arterial. I, on the other hand, have no such heart, or smile, or purity. Jacko's eyes on me are a part of every song. We jam for an hour.

You're letting loose tonight, feeling the music, really getting down. But, out of vanity, you're not wearing your glasses. I bet you couldn't recognize me in my yearbooks, even with the whole face there. And you don't feel sorry for the fruit bats, tricked by artificial dusk and the promise of a long, full night ahead.

You say, "That's all they know, honey. All these animals. They think this is how it's supposed to be."

**WHEN LOVEY FOUND OUT** that I activated our baby without her, she was pretty choked.

"We were going to be together when it happened," she said, in her little voice. "I had my outfit, the candles, the aromatherapy—"

"I couldn't wait," I told her. "The waiting was killing me." All of this was on the phone, over which she could hear the baby screaming its newborn lungs out—a healthy sign, the instructions said, let it cry for at least 3 minutes and no more than ten. We were up to four and a half.

"It wasn't killing you," she said softly. "You just hate to wait. I thought we were on the same page about this. After all we've been through."

"It was worse than knowing where my presents are and not opening them," I said. "Worse than waiting for my father's estate to be settled. I'm sorry, Lovey. I just had to go ahead."

She started crying a little. "I'm not mad about your enthusiasm. I just wanted to be there. I wanted to, you know, be a part of it."

"You wanted to help. I should have waited." I was a schmuck. I know. Since when does a woman not want to be present at the activation of her child? It happens, of course, people do it alone, but it wasn't in our plans. We were supposed to be together.

To be honest, I didn't want her help with this one. This one was going to be mine, although of course, we would share it 50/50: the diapers, the sling-wearing, the high-pitched babbling. Secretly, though, all mine.

"What's wrong with me, Henry? Do you think I couldn't handle it, you know, if…"

"Nothing's wrong with you," I lied. "I love you."

I do love her. But I also know what she ate for dinner last night, at her favourite Greek cantina. No one wants a garlic-scented baby. That smell can hang around for weeks—even Pampers can't disguise it.

There's something else, too. Her voice drives me batty. She is so soft-spoken I can barely hear her. It's not a mumbling thing: I've dealt with that in my time. This is volume, pure and simple. She speaks to everyone just above whisper-level. Do you think I wanted to pass that onto our son? Have you ever met a man who speaks like a mouse? Did you want to give him a job, or marry him, or even sit beside him on the bus? I don't think so.

"Is there something wrong with us, then?"

I groaned. "Honey, I've gotta go. The baby is freaking out. And the booklet says—"

"Okay," she said. "I'll see you at five."

Then I remembered why the baby might be crying. "Wait!" I yelled into the phone just before she hung up. "Can you pick up some formula? It only came with one can and it's almost empty."

"Okay," she said. "But aren't you even going tell me?"

"What?"

She was speaking so softly I could barely make out her voice over the baby.

"Well?" she asked. "Boy or girl?"

"Congratulations, momma," I said. "You've got a baby boy."

She hung up without saying a thing. At least I think she did. All I heard was the baby.

**WE'D BEEN WAITING FOR MONTHS** for the package to arrive, after finally going through the second screening. But this morning, there it was on the front porch, an unmarked brown box like the one the sex toys came in the year I surprised Lovey for her birthday. I think the risk the company takes in not marking the boxes is considerable, the way the mailman just leaves them on the steps like that. I know there are people out there who are desperate to get their hands on this kind of product. Yet the privacy is worth it: even though we're not ashamed to be doing this, even though it's a perfectly viable means to an end, still, people have a problem with it. One day, no one will care whether you came from a box or a uterus. But we're not there yet.

The package is only part of the recipe. Actually creating the finished product takes a certain amount of skill and intention. In fact, many people say that the intention may be the biggest part of it, thinking good thoughts as your baby comes to life right in front of you. There are books out there now on what to meditate on when the big moment comes, including DVDs attached to the back cover that will play scenes of rustic beauty while you make your child come to life. There are others, too, of a woman giving birth, the old way, because some people believe that hearing the screams of a mother in pain does something good to a baby's ears, that it simulates what a birthed baby would hear. I don't get it. Aren't we trying to get away from all of that?

(We bought a book about Provence, France, that came with a bottle of lavender and a classical music CD attached, but I completely forgot where we put it. Instead I chose some electronica to get me in the groove. Like I said, my baby.)

Once the package came, we were going to wait until the timing was perfect. Set the mood, prepare ourselves, turn the heat on in the nursery, gather our spit over a few hours to make sure it had variety. We were going to collect it in a beautiful bowl, stir it together, let it mix well before adding the boiling water and sprinkling in the powder that would work its way into becoming our son.

Instead, I produced massive amounts of my own saliva and measured it into a Tupperware cup. The recipe had an optional ingredient, and since I had nothing to lose, no one to dispute it with, yes, I added my own "juice" to the mix. I'm not sure if it's true that it increases the chances of giving us a boy, but that's what I wanted. I figured it was worth a shot, so to speak. And look. Just look at this little guy.

**HERE'S SOMETHING YOU SHOULD KNOW.** We were selected a few years ago for the program, and we had a little girl. We did all the right things: rituals, blessings, friends gathered at the window while we stirred the pot, but she didn't make it, not even past the first five minutes. We thought it was us, something we had done to make it go wrong, but everyone told us it wasn't our fault. "Bad things happen to good people" was written on about five cards we received that week. There was no one to blame. When we found out a year later about the faulty packaging, once the law suits began piling up against IF 1-2-3, we considered filing suit ourselves. But we'd been through enough. And, we wanted to try again. What company would let someone have another chance with its product if he'd taken them to the cleaners in a courtroom? We grieved in private for our little one, barely here and then gone. Genny was her name, chosen months before. We grieved, and then waited for our second go.

This little one is feisty, I'll give him that. Right away he was screaming, opening his eyes, waving his little fists around like he already had a problem with the world. I have to tell you, the sound of his loud cries was music to my ears, living as I do with a quiet freak. Once I got the feeding device strapped onto my chests and the formula flowing from the silicone nipple, he settled right down. Will he remember this, our first moments together? Will I imprint on him the way I'm supposed to, the way a parent did in the pre-IF days? Will we pass the first stage of assessment? Will we see this little guy off to school one day? Will we really, truly be his parents, the ones he calls Mom and Dad and loves and then hates and then loves again?

The first check-in is supposed to be within the first week after activation. If the baby seems happy, healthy, if the APGAR ratings are good and he's settling when we pick him up, then we get to keep him. The next check-in is at one year. Most parents keep their babies for good if they make it past that one. That's the one we have to ace.

**FROM MY STATION ON THE COUCH** I can see outside, but no one can see me. It's perfect. I'm not ready to have the world involved in my little project.

From here I can see Judy Taylor, our next-door neighbour, walking down the street. She's out of her pyjamas, finally. Poor lady. She's been through so much. I've been catching glimpses of her through their kitchen window, from our kitchen window, and most of the time, she looks like she's just rolled out of bed.

I've been looking for work lately. I take my time with the dishwashing.

She's looking this way, checking for signs of someone being home. Shit. I'm not prepared for visitors yet. Walk on by, Judy. Walk on by.

Thank you, Judy.

Judy and Derek got their first IF 1-2-3 box a few months ago, back when a weird weather pattern came through and the snow was piling up everywhere like feathers. They were so worried the box had been outside too long, since they both work and didn't get home to bring it in until 6 pm. If only they'd asked me, I would've helped out. In any case, everything seemed fine, and they went through the steps, and then, out came twin girls. That was a shock, to say the least. IF 1-2-3 has taken great care to ensure that babies come in singles these days, after one family ended up with three identical instant girls.

It's funny, but no one can seem to handle multiples these days, not like they did twenty years ago. Everyone who couldn't conceive went to incredible lengths to get an embryo implanted inside them, and the hormones they took made the number of multiple births skyrocket. That's why people started turning to IF instead. The price of raising three kids at once is only one factor, of course. The complications from birthing a baby were getting everyone worked up. I pity the poor midwives, who'd just gotten their profession really rolling when IF came along. Now they're calling themselves Re-con-Naissance workers, hiring themselves out to nervous families to ease the worries about activation and those first few vital days. We thought we might hire one this time, after what happened before, but in the end, we thought we'd rather do it on our own. Guess I took that to a whole new level. I really should call Lovey and apologize.

Anyway, Judy's twins seemed fine, eating and pooping at regular intervals, holding fingers in their fists, drooling with red cheeks during the first teething phase. The first week check-in officer took a healthy bribe to make sure the news of having two didn't make it back to the corporation and everything was going well. Then, at five months, one of those black IF vans pulled into the driveway, and within minutes, the babies were being strapped into carpods in the backseat. Judy was running after the van as it drove away, holding out two pink teddy bears. They won't sleep without them! she cried. They're Lullaby Bear-Bears! She collapsed on the sidewalk and stayed there until her husband rushed out to take her back inside.

It took us a few days to figure out what had happened. It turns out the package they'd received in the mail wasn't meant for them, but instead should have gone to Mango Waterson, the one-woman musical wonder. It was all one big mix-up. Mango had secretly paid IF 1-2-3 a huge amount of cash to give her a set of twins they had prevented from going into circulation. She wanted to have two kids the way her mother did, but she didn't want to wait between them, given her touring schedule and so on. It's maddening what that kind of money can do for you. IF itself is pricey, let me tell you, but to have them work on your own special case costs a fortune.

Our neighbour has plenty of cash now, after IF agreed to pay for psychological damages, and she's been promised one of the new models as soon as they work the bugs out. I imagine she'll be coming over here a lot, once she hears about our little son.

Perhaps we can even help Judy out: with the price of the recommended water to mix with the formula, it will be cheaper to pay her to nurse him. Once the milk starts flowing, it's easier to just keep it going than stop and start again. Lovey didn't even get started with Genny. It takes a few days for the lactation hormones to kick in, and even then, the latching takes awhile to master. That's why this strapon set of breasts is ingenious. I can be a mommy just like the next guy. I just stay away from the window.

**YOU THINK IT'S WRONG, DON'T YOU?** At first everyone here thought the idea of IF was preposterous, too. Babies aren't soup, or orange juice, the cries went up. Babies need a slow percolation in utero to develop in the way they were meant to. Ah, meaning, intention, the argument always came back to the *natural* state of things. Burning oil felt natural but was it? Global warming felt pretty natural, just like weather, until we couldn't ignore it anymore. Were the water shortages, and the ensuing madness, natural? No. We do what we can to survive. We are creative beings. Just because the blood of his mother—or any mother, directly—did not flow through him, does not make my son any less human.

Besides, how they do it is just like how a body does it. The fateful meeting of sperm and ovum from anonymous, highly-screened donors occurs in a controlled environment—and then replication takes over. The lab watches until the embryo stage is complete, at 10 weeks, and then, after some secret patented process, they freeze-dry and powder the embryos under strict controls. No one is hurt, nothing is lost, and everyone who wants a baby gets one, in the end. As long as they're deemed to be suitable, of course. Do you know what that's done for the morale of single women over 35? Do you have any idea how many marriages, not to mention egos, vaginas, and flat bellies have been saved? I don't have the numbers, they won't let that information out at this point, but I know this city alone is crawling with IF babies. No pun intended.

Lovey wanted to do it the old way. At first, she was totally against this system, but we won't tell that to our new son, now will we? I went along with it, of course, I mean, trying to get a woman pregnant is not such a bad way to spend your time, and we've got a decent set of bones between us. But I knew the risks, and the odds. I wanted to do it the new way. I wanted to save us all the trouble.

Then, when Genny didn't last, Lovey had more doubts. She's quite set in her ways, you know, with her all-recycled wardrobe and her beeswax-only candle rule. I don't miss paraffin in the least, but she's not even willing to try the new, cheaper hybrid candles. I'm not exactly fond of the idea of burning rat fat in the house either, but you do what you need to. Now, with the baby, that isn't going to happen, ever. I'll bet she won't even let me run the environmental simulator inside anymore. There's no way she'll want to smell peanut butter cookies baking. You're missing the point, she'll say. Peanuts kill children. Why would I want to even fake that?

**MY BOY IS ASLEEP NOW, FINALLY.** I'd put him in the cradle but I don't want to wake him up. And I like the warmth of him, his little chest pushing into mine with every breath. Once Lovey gets home, I know she'll want to take over, which is the mothering instinct kicking in. She'll want to strap the milk machine on right away. She'll want to sing him her family lullaby in that sweet annoying voice, to try and lull him into believing that he came from her womb.

Can't say I blame her. It's weird, but when I look at him, this boy, this newly sprung creature lying in my arms, I swear I see my sister's eyes starting back at me. The manual says that's natural, to see resemblances where there are none: after all, how much genetic material can be transferred through spit? I know the old double-helix trick does not come from blending semen with saliva in a bowl in some kitchen by a man standing all alone. But still—it might be an energetic thing. It might even be magic.

He's awake again, squirming in my arms, trying to tell me something. "You wanna watch television?" I ask him in the quiet, tender tone they recommend talking in for the first year. "You wanna meet your Daddy's favourite team?"

He lets out a wail so loud I nearly drop him. Atta boy. "Okay, so no baseball," I say, and I plug him back into the silicone boob. He's a smart little guy, he latches on again right away and swallows great big mouthfuls of milk without choking. At this rate, we're going to be out of formula long before my wife gets home with more. The package came with a recipe in case of such emergencies but I doubt we have half of the ingredients. Who stocks dried egg whites anymore? Who has extra ionically-charged water to mix them with? And soy milk. You think I want genetically modified ingredients in my son? Luckily this stuff he's drinking now seems to knock him out after only a few minutes. This time, I'm going to try and put him down on the couch so I can get cleaned up before my wife gets home.

But before I can do that, I hear a car in the driveway. So she's come home early, unable to wait. That's my girl. She—

The doorbell is ringing. Shit. It's not her. And we made a promise that we wouldn't tell anyone about the next one until we were sure he/ she was going to make it. If I put him down, he might start freaking out. If I don't, how will I ever disguise a strap-on set of breasts and a wiggling newborn?

I'm not answering. Instead I go into the kitchen to spy out the window.

It's not a car in the driveway. It's a flipping IF1-2-3 van. What the hell are they doing here? They don't usually visit until at least a week after the activation—and I haven't even notified them yet. Unless. Unless they've known from the first second. Are they spying on me right now? Shit! Or maybe this baby is a new model and has some kind of sensor in him. Oh God. What am I going to do now?

They're knocking. There are at least two, because I can hear them talking to each other. I sneak back into the hallway so I can hear what they're saying. The baby is still sleeping, thank god.

"Hello?" one of them, a man, says. "Mr. and Mrs. Taylor?"

I don't answer.

A woman's voice now: "We're from IF headquarters. We're just here to welcome the baby, friends. Would you mind letting us in?"

Another pause. I hold my breath.

"It's very important that we see you, friends. We are required to make visual contact with the child before reporting back. If we don't, we're required to obtain a search warrant for your house. You don't want that, do you?"

I don't move.

"Damn," the guy says, in a quieter voice, "maybe they're out for a walk or something."

"No," the woman says. "I know they're here."

"No car in the driveway."

"So maybe one of them is at work."

"That's weird, then. Activating a kid by yourself."

"I know. But it wouldn't be the first time." She pumps up her voice. "Mr. and Mrs. Taylor, we just want to congratulate you on the arrival of your son. May we please come in for a moment? We have a gift for you that we can't leave outside." She pounds on the door to punctuate her statement.

Of course, the baby wakes up. I try to cover his face up, but he yells, rather than cries, as if he's mad to be taken out of a beautiful dream state. What do babies dream about, anyway? How will we ever know?

"Aha!" I hear the woman say. "I hear a baby in there," she says down at mail slot level.

"Congratulations!" the man calls out. "You're going to be very happy. Now may we please come in to give you this gift?"

Now the baby is really crying. I slip the nipple into his mouth to quiet him. "No, thank you," I say. "We're doing fine. I'll call to set up the first visit."

"Sir," the woman says. "We're afraid you'll have to do as we say."

Just as she starts banging on the door again, I hear another car pull in. This time, I know it's my wife.

I run to the kitchen phone to call her cell. She answers right away.

"Honey!" I say. "These people want to come in. I didn't even tell them we made the baby yet, they just knew!"

"What's wrong? Who are they? What's wrong with them coming in?"

I make myself take a deep breath. "Just stay in the car talking to me. Smile at them, make them think you're talking to someone else."

"Okay," she says. "I just waved at them. Are they from IF?"

"That's what they say."

"Well, how did they know about it? You didn't call them? Did anyone see you with the baby?" Her voice is so mild, it's like we're talking about the frigging weather.

"No, no. There must be some kind of sensor. I know as much as you do. But I don't trust them. They want to give us a gift of some kind."

"I can see a box beside the woman. A big box of diapers."

"Diapers! It's probably some kind of spy device in disguise."

"I'm telling you, it's a carton of Pampers. Are you all right?"

"Jesus. So that's what they're afraid to leave on the porch? I guess they are worth a few bucks, but who would think to steal a man's box of diapers?"

"Honey, I'm getting out of the car now. I'll talk to you inside."

And before she hears me yelling at her to stop, she hangs up.

I take up station in the kitchen, on the floor, so I can hear everything from the screen window. I can hear my wife getting out of the car.

"Hello," the IF woman says to her. "You must be Mrs. Taylor." I can picture her sticking out her manicured paw for my wife to shake, to assure her that everything is just fine. "Congratulations on your son."

"Hi, Mrs. Taylor!" The man says it like he's talking to a toddler, saying peek-a-boo.

I strain to hear my wife's voice. "I'm sorry," she says, which is just like her. "Did you say Taylor?"

"Yes, Mrs. Taylor, right? You just activated your son?"

And what my wife is doing right now I do not know, but I can imagine. I can picture her starting to shake her head, and stop walking towards our door, but look at it, like the door might give her the answer she suddenly is in need of, namely, why is this woman calling her by the neighbour's name?

"You have the wrong house," she says, quietly. "The Taylors are next door." At this she must be pointing towards the rusty brown house beside us—why anyone would even think of painting their house that colour is beyond me anyway—and I'll bet you her confusion is slowly being turned into realization, yes, she must be putting two and two together, she's good at that, she—

"Really?" the woman says. "But there's a baby inside your house, correct?"

My wife lets out some kind of noise I've never heard before, a cross between a hiccup and a gasp that I can only call a sob, although I have always thought of sob as only a verb, as in "to sob." She knows what I've done.

I've activated the Taylors' baby.

"What is going on here?" the man says, in a tone of put-on authority. A hands-on hips, park ranger voice.

My wife is crying now, really sobbing, albeit quietly, and I can feel the baby start to stir in my arms again, as if he's already attuned to the world's sadness, his mother's distress, waking up in her time of need even though he hasn't even met her yet.

"I don't have the foggiest," the IF woman says. "But all I know is that the baby in this house was activated at 2:35 pm today and that we're here to ensure that it meets all of our current standards. And, of course, to bring the parents a little gift."

"But where is Mrs. Taylor?" the man asks my wife. "Is she in your house with the baby? I am sure, given the unfortunate circumstances of the duplicate activation and removal, that she might want to have it elsewhere. We understand that's what neighbours do, Mrs....?"

My wife is still crying, but eventually she says our last name with as much dignity as she can, given the circumstances. "Peterson."

And once again, the baby puts forth a yell that startles me into nearly dropping him before he settles into a nice general sort of crying.

Someone is banging on the door. "Mr. Peterson," the man is shouting. "Would you and Mrs. Taylor please come out here now. And bring the baby."

I slip the nipple into his mouth yet again and all is quiet.

I did all of this for Lovey. I did. I knew she wouldn't be able to handle the Taylors having another baby, not after what happened to ours. Not after failing the screening.

No, okay, so we *didn't* make it through a second time. It was just because of a stupid traffic violation I had in Chicago. Anyone could have done it. A baby in a carpod would NOT have been hurt, at least nothing more than a few bruises. "Higher than acceptable risk factors" was how they put it on the rejection slip. If Lovey had been home to get the mail that day, she would've been destroyed. Luckily I have no employment at the present. Luckily I am always home to accept the mail. Luckily, I am able to watch for deliveries to all of our neighbours' houses.

"I'll go see if Mrs. Taylor is in there," my wife says, sniffling. "Maybe I could go in and bring the baby out, if she's nervous."

"All right," the man says. "But we're going to have to call in backup if you're not out in five minutes. This is a serious matter, Mrs. Peterson. We need a visual affirmation."

My wife's key is in the door. Lovey, the new mother on the block. Lovey, the woman I have given my life to, so that we may go forth and create new life. The woman I have betrayed and stolen for, in order for us to have this wittle boy. Thanks to IF 1-2-3—and their ridiculous shipping policies—we have had our second chance.

When she sees us on the floor beside the kitchen table she drops her purse and the shopping bags. The cans of formula hit the lino with a considerable thunk—I know they're going to be dented—and the baby startles with the sound and twitches as if he's been hit but he keeps on nursing. Lovey's crying again, and when she slides to the floor and joins us, and fits her finger into the little guy's grasp, I just feel the happiest I have ever felt.

"Congratulations, momma," I whisper, as I hand my son to her.

"Oh, honey, what have you done?" She's not looking at me, only into the eyes of this newborn, nameless child. "Why couldn't you have waited for our own package?"

"What do you mean?" I ask her, pretending one last time. "I've made us a baby, all by myself."

THE JEALOUSY BONE

Now she's looking at me. "They called me Mrs. Taylor. What kind of deal did you make with her?"

"Deal? No deal. She doesn't know a thing."

Lovey looks slightly relieved, then stricken. "But she'll want her baby. We can't keep him."

"He's *ours*," I tell her. "Mine, anyway. He's got my seed in him."

She stares at me. "Don't you ever tell that to Mrs. Taylor."

"She's not getting him."

She wipes tears from her face. "We've got four minutes before they're taking him," she says. "That's three more than we had with Genny."

I can't believe this. My own wife is going to betray me. After what I've done for her. She doesn't realize what this might mean. Jail time, probably, and then where will she be, except alone in this house with no baby or husband and a connection to crime. IF 1-2-3 would never give her a second glance.

She kisses the baby on the cheek. "It won't be long until we get our own."

"We didn't pass the screening."

I've never seen that look she's giving me. It's like one side of her face is being built and the other is falling down. The tears come back. "So there is something wrong with us."

"No, nothing. They're just wankers."

"Was it your accident? Is that it?"

I ignore her deduction. "This is our last chance!" I say. "Unless... Yes, I've got it! We find the sensor and remove it."

She shakes her head. "How do you even know there's a sensor?"

"There has to be. They worked out a new formula, remember? If we destroy it, they'll think the baby has died."

The IF man bangs on the door again. "Two minutes, Mrs. Peterson."

"You're going crazy," Lovey says. "We have to give him back."

"Give him to me. I'll find the stupid sensor and take it out myself." I reach out and try to grasp the baby around the middle, but Lovey pulls him away before I can catch hold.

"No!" Lovey screams as she gets up and runs towards the door. "You'll hurt the baby!"

The baby is screaming now, too, but it's Lovey's yelling that surprises me. She hasn't raised her voice like that in years. It's healthy, I always tell her. You've got to let it out. I just can't, she says. I wasn't born with that kind of wiring.

Apparently, she was. "Wait!" I say. "I have another plan."

I know my wife. I know she'll stop before getting to the door, because she is—

"What's going on in there?" the IF woman calls. "We're calling for backup now, Petersons."

—desperate to have a baby. Yes, she wants to do what's right, but she wants a baby more.

"Take the baby to the window and show them he's okay. While you're doing that, I'll get the bikes out of the shed, and we can leave down the back lane."

She looks at me. I look at her. The baby is crying, but she's started that rocking motion that I've seen parents do, a jiggling with their legs and arms at the same time to bounce them into calming down. It's working. "Nice one, mama," I say. "He likes you."

Slowly, a smile starts compiling itself on her face. "You really think this will work?"

I have no idea. Bike against van is never a winning situation, but we've got to try something. And what kind of father would I be if I didn't at least try to save my own son? Selfish, that's what. "Look at that baby," I tell her. "He's got your nose."

# CHICORY

**THREE DAYS AGO, ANOTHER CAT.** Dani didn't want another cat. It had only been a few months since the last one had died, put to sleep because of feline leukemia. Too much suffering, she had insisted to James, her ex-husband, and I for one don't want to watch a slow death. The marriage was over, by this point, over after only a few years, and had there ever been happiness? Hills and valleys, a few peaks, mostly a flat, dull road, trailing off into the bush. They had been twenty-three when they wed. Who even gets married at that age anymore?

No one they knew but them, and look at where they were.

**WHERE SHE WAS** was in Mexico, *healing* from all of this, taking time to figure things out, making space in her life for new growth. She was, as her mother had suggested, *putting herself out there*, although if her mother knew exactly what this entailed, she would not think it was a good idea. She was renting a green and pink house, pink on the inside and green on the out, making her the little watermelon seed, on a back street in a fishing village cum ex-pat artists' enclave called Todos Santos. She was taking a leave of absence from being a federal government drone to test out her line of credit, pretend to paint pathetic watercolours, drink tequila and beer every night and bring home men of varying pedigree: travellers and wealthy artists and surfers.

She cared only that they be different from James. So far, no post-men with wide-spaced teeth and tears in their eyes half the time. No men spitting on the ground as they walked to give penance to the plants they were crushing. No men wearing bulbous leather pouches full of gemstones around their neck, summoning the spirits of sun and sky. Luck had been with her so far. She hadn't seen a single smudging bundle or Animal medicine card. Putting herself out there had proved easier than she would ever have imagined. She attracted men like ants to a trail of mango juice.

**THREE DAYS AGO, A KITTEN STARED AT HER** from across the road. It was minuscule, half the size of one of the running shoes she was tying before her run. I see you, she said to the kitten. Just stay where you are. But once she was off her porch, walking past, the grey smidgen of a cat came out from under its rusted Pontiac shelter and blared its eyes at her. Its fur was matted, one ear mangled, it was covered in flea bites, but none of these detracted from the kitten's eyes. They were the blue of silk lining, and of chicory, the weeds Dani picked as a child. The flowers always closed up their round blue faces once she picked them, but she yanked them from the ground anyway. The kitten sat there, in the early morning sun, trying to groom itself. She felt her resolve begin to melt. It wasn't like she was against *cats*, per se...

No. She was there temporarily. She was there selfishly. She was there to get over the past. No more cats.

She took off on her run into the desert along a trail between cacti and heaps of rusted cans, towards Punta Lobos, the beach where the fishermen launched their *pangas* into the rolling sea. The last time she ran this trail, she'd caught a glimpse of a young man on an ATV, jerking off behind one of the dunes. She didn't disturb him. She just picked up her pace. When she got to the beach, she took off her shoes and socks and waded in the water, letting the waves suck at her calves. Then she climbed to the top of the concrete lighthouse for a view of the beach and the town. Evidence of loving and drunken bliss littered the stairs. Not her choice for a rendezvous, but as soon as she thought this, she imagined bringing Lang here, pressing his butt against the cool cement, doing what everyone else had done.

**LANG WAS A THREAD** woven through her Mexican adventure, a brightly coloured cross-strand. He was a mountain biker, sponsored by sports companies she recognized to train in the Baja for the winter. He lived at the beach with his pothead trainer in a small RV. When he wasn't riding he was surfing, and when he wasn't surfing he was getting high. He was an ex-marine, an ex-body-piercing model, an ex-husband, not much older than Dani. Yes, he had been pierced *down there*. Most of his rings were out now, and the holes were starting to grow over, except for the ones he kept up. Maintenance of a piercing was essential to its use, he told her the first night they were together, when he asked her to feed a twist-tie through one of his nipples.

I could stretch those holes in your lobes big enough to look through, he told her.

She felt both earlobes, the little BBs she could roll in her fingertips where the earring gun had pierced her so long ago. She thought of the song, Do your ears hang low?

I'm good for now, she said.

But had she been good half an hour before? After she invited him back to her place for a drink, after drinking at the bar-restaurant where they'd met on the dance floor, the two of them had lined up shots on her kitchen counter, a bit of Jose Cuervo in every cup she owned. He was the one who suggested the body shots, the first to lick her neck, sprinkle it with salt, then shove a wedge of lime between her lips before licking the salt off again, shooting the tequila and sucking the lime from her mouth. She was so enamoured, she thought it was something he'd invented. When it was her turn, she couldn't stop her mouth at the lime. He undressed as they kissed, and pulled her into the bedroom.

His whole body was brown, and shaven from chest to feet. She let her hands explore up and down, over his smooth testicles, his penis with its slight curve, his flat belly. She let his hands undress her, a quick yank of her sundress over her head, a thumbslide under the cotton of her thong and then a tug to rip them off.

Good was not a term she associated with any of what they got up to. Words she had never heard aloud before were directed at *her*, and she liked it. When he asked if he could pour hot wax on her belly, she said no. He smiled at her and said, I'll ask again in a week. She held onto the twist tie and pulled, hard.

After, he said, Give me your hand.

She sat beside him and held out her right hand. He used her index finger to trace a route over his body, from hole to scar to hole, connecting the dots and dashes, and as he did this, he told her a little about each one. She closed her eyes and felt his voice inside her, low and dark. Whatever he was saying didn't really register: only when he stopped talking did she open her eyes, and only then did she see his cock, standing tall again.

Following that night, it was hit and miss. They had an agreement of sorts: to meet up casually, to rely on circumstance and fate, to assume no exclusivity. She knew where he bought his groceries: who didn't shop at the government-subsidized grocery store, where alcohol, tuna and toilet paper were cheaper than anywhere else? He knew where she liked to eat her lunch, in the old sugar mill, or in the *huerta* under the avocado trees, where she sometimes smeared a few

THE JEALOUSY BONE

tropical splashes of paint onto paper, trying to play the part. He would ask her to do things; she didn't always say yes, and most of the time, he didn't push her. So far, the set-up was working out.

**ON THE WAY HOME FROM THE BEACH** she ran a different path along a rutted road in the sand, passing empty shells of cars and eaten-out skeletons of birds. She rounded a turn and came to a sudden stop. There, across her path, was a dead dog. It was not a recent death. This dog was sun-dried, flattened, thin as a magazine. The elements had had their way with it, and no one had bothered to even move it from the trail. James came into her head then, the sorrow he would have felt if he had found this poor beast. He would have dug a grave for it in the sand, with his hands if he had to, ceremoniously buried the dog, incanting blessings over its dehydrated body. He would have imagined white light around it, easing its transition into the next life.

Dani jumped over the carcass and ran under the relentless sun. It was rising to near-noon, turning the day into another like the one before, hot and dry. It had not rained in her four months there. She dreamt of rain nearly every night, the forests of the cool Pacific Northwest, mist from a heavy grey sky. This was one of the few things she missed. Rain and muffins and decent cheese. She ran as fast as she could, feeling the sweat collecting in her short hair before running down her neck; she pretended it was falling from the sky.

At the corner store she stopped to buy eggs, placing them into a plastic bag like walnuts, loose, rolling. She had missed the daily line-up at the *tortilleria*, where she showed the girl how many corn tortillas she wanted by measuring an imaginary stack between her thumb and fingers, but she still had a few left in the fridge from the day before. Her new staple: salsa, avocado, and scrambled egg burrito. She held the eggs away from her body and jogged down the street.

Lang was sitting on her porch, drinking a Tecate. The kitten slept beside him, curled up like a snail.

*Hola*, he said, in his eastern seaboard accent. Nice *huevos*.

Nice pussy, she said. But don't get any ideas.

I was just in the neighbourhood.

So was the cat. You want to come in for some protein?

I was going to ask you the same thing. Lang grabbed his crotch and wiggled his eyebrows.

She thought of the joke from high school sex ed. The innocent question from the prom queen, who asks, when told that semen is mostly sugar and protein, But why does it taste so salty?

For dessert, she said. But the kitten stays out here.

While she fried the eggs, Lang tried to convince her to take the cat in. It will die if you don't, he said. Too many damn dogs around here. There were dogs everywhere; dogs that appeared dead during the day in front of houses, the butcher's, the taco stand, strewn like forgotten toys; dogs that only came to life when the sun disappeared. On the rare occasions when she walked home alone at night, she walked with rocks in her hands.

He got her to help him bathe the cat, and cracked open an egg to feed it. The cat wasn't interested. Dani ran back to the store for a box of Kitten Chow, but it was too young even for that. Eventually, with some milk, they got it purring.

Come on, he said. You know you want it.

I don't. I don't want a pet right now.

He grabbed her hands and wrapped them around his waist. Pet for a pet. It's just temporary, he said. You can find him a home before you leave.

She felt herself sinking into him, his supple muscles like a mattress, like something she needed more than this time away, or the margaritas, or the paint box scenery in town. James had never felt this way to her. How do you dissolve into scaffolding? How do you relax into bone?

Are you trying to get rid of me? she asked.

Yeah, that's why I'm suggesting this cat thing. That's why I'm here. He pinched her butt cheek, something James had never done either.

Lang had preferences. His curvy penis hit her in places she hadn't been hit before. He liked to hit her, too, little slaps, when the timing was right. Despite their laissez-faire arrangement, she thought of him and what she wanted to do with him every day, and casually kept her eyes peeled while she walked. Blindfolds, rope, dirty words all filled her head in the middle of the day, and at night, kept her awake. There were still things she wouldn't let him do, but she was a long way from lying on her back thinking of the light fixtures.

Dani smiled. All right. But you have to help me find it a home, when the time comes.

Deal. He licked her right ear.

Dani set up a shoe box as a cat bed in the second bedroom, then carried the kitten to it. She gently closed the door.

Happy? she asked Lang, who was in her bedroom, folding her old blue bandanna into a blindfold.

Yeah. Lang looked at her with his head tilted. You'd look good with a nose ring.

I had one, she said. I took it out too soon, and it grew over. She held one of his brown, roughened hands in hers, then drew his middle finger over the tiny indentation on the left side of her nose, the way he had done with her their first night together. She thought of the lighthouse again, pressing him up against the cool sides of the inner wall, the rough edges of the window ledge digging into his ass, leaving their mark.

Come here, he said, and tugged her closer to him. His mouth was open when they kissed. His eyes were clear today. She felt herself responding, returning the energy, happy, despite their agreement, that he had sought her out at home.

I'm all sweaty, she said. I should have a shower.

No, Lang said. He pulled her t-shirt off and licked her chest. *Muy bien.*

Then the meowing began.

Ignore it, Lang said. I've got something you'll like better.

Maybe it needs to pee.

It's a wild animal. It's not trained yet.

The cat wouldn't stop.

Well, maybe it's stuck.

Lang sighed. All right, go.

It wasn't stuck, but two puddles were merging on the cement floor beside the shoebox, and the cat was scratching at its head. She lifted the cat up carefully, worried about the sores on its fur, and put it outside.

Get back here, Lang called.

I just have to wash my hands.

By the time she was back in the bedroom, stopping to admire Lang's naked body lain out on her sheets, the cat was meowing again.

For fuck's sake, he said.

It was your idea, she said. Just a sec.

Dani let the cat back in, and closed it in the second bedroom again.

Okay, she said, let's do this. She stripped off her panties.

Get on. He held his cock upright, stroking it to bring it back to attention.

Let me get the belt, she said. The last time, he had asked her to strangle him while he came. It had been surprising, his response, the intensity of his orgasm, the way he took so long to focus on her afterwards, as if he had gone somewhere far away.

No, he said. Use your hands. Then he slapped her on the ass. The cry she made sounded just like the meowing.

No, that *was* meowing. They managed to ignore it long enough to finish the job, with no time for the blindfold or anything else but the basics. Both of them got up right away, and after a quick pat to the kitten's mangy head Lang was gone, saying something about meeting his buddy at the beer depot.

Shit. What had she said about no cats?

**THE HOURS UNTIL NIGHTFALL** were a comical in-again, out-again dance. Dani was exhausted by the time the sun set. For once she was grateful for the ranchero music floating over from the Lion's hall, because it drowned out the sound of the meowing cat. After three hours, the music was over, and the cat was still at it. She put it outside again. Then, the neighbours' dog started barking. She stuck her head out and saw the cat, stuck in a tiny spot beside the water heater, alternating between crying and hissing at the frantic dog.

Come here, you little scrap, she called from the back door. The cat was terrified, rooted to the spot. The dog kept barking and growling viciously, overtaken by instinct, a dog she had been wary of since moving into the house, even though it was small and homely. An ankle-biter of some kind; a rat killer.

Get lost! she shouted. *Vamonos.* At this, the dog might have lifted his head, but it was for only half a second. She didn't know any other Spanish dog commands, aside from *Aqui,* and she didn't want that beast anywhere near her. The cat was mashed up against the metal gas canister for the water heater, certain to die if it fell over.

She grabbed a broom and ran down the steps. Grrrr! she shouted, stomping her feet. The neighbours' light came on, and the teenaged boy of the house stood at the door and called the dog inside. This boy was the same one who played the soundtrack of *Titanic* at full blast during the week she was in bed with bronchitis, until she complained to his mother. He had a look of satisfaction on his sleepy face as he held the door for his idiotic dog.

The cat was bloody, its fur was mangled, its eyes were swollen half-shut. It breathed with a heavy wheeze, as if it had punctured a lung. Dani brought it inside, put it in the shoebox, and kept vigil for the rest of the night, listening for breathing, both relieved and distraught at the same time when she heard it. The kitten was suffering.

Her thoughts were on a repeat cycle, coming back to one question: what would James have done this time? A dried-out dog was one thing. But a dying stray cat? When their beloved Max had to be put down James had wept for days, claiming that he had taken on their marital strife like a sponge, claiming it was a symbol of their relationship. To Dani, all it meant was that they had been too busy fighting to notice how sick their cat had become. For this kitten James would call in the big guns, although he would never use that term: throw salt in the four corners of the house, cleanse the wall where the damage was done, hold the injured cat in his palms, put a net of healing over the whole neighbourhood.

And where the hell was Lang, anyway? It was more his cat than hers. His brilliant idea. He ought to take a shift or two.

By morning the cat was still breathing, but only once every thirty seconds. Dani alternated between staring at it and pacing, back door to front and back again, trying to figure out what to do. She kept the curtains closed. She didn't run out to the orange seller's truck when he drove past her door. She didn't dare to have a shower until the afternoon, when she was nearly passing out from the heat and fatigue.

When she came out of the shower, the kitten was dead.

This time tears came, and in them a longing for James that she hadn't felt since leaving, a release valve on everything she had put away to deal with later. She was lonely. What was she doing, getting hit while making love? Did she really want to strangle her lover while he came?

She picked up the kitten and wrapped it in her bandanna, and rocked its swaddled body in her arms.

**IT TOOK HER UNTIL THE EVENING TO CALM DOWN,** with the rest of Lang's six-pack to help. Dani tried to dig a grave for the kitten with a spoon because she couldn't bear to ask to borrow a shovel from her neighbours. She carved into the inch of dust under one of the lime trees and struck compacted, stubborn, rock-hard earth. She needed a shovel. She set the wrapped-up cat onto the ground and went back inside to search for something else to use.

The light outside was starting to mellow, and five children with a loop of garden hose screamed outside her window, their feet thudding the dirt street as they ran to catch one another with their black and green lasso. A military man in training strolled the barbed wire fence across from her house, looking into the fruit trees as if into a face. He had blossoms in his shiny black hair. On her side of the street, yellow morning glories grew over the car battery and beer bottles at the bottom of the fence, their trumpets closed until morning. Green birds that looked like limes with wings jumped in the vines, then flew to the lime trees. The wind died down with the sun. Three young men were walking towards the graveyard, singing, while one of them played a guitar. The dog across the street, the only one tied up for blocks, barked and whimpered to be free. Another night in the village was beginning. It would not be quiet until four am, and then only for a moment, until the roosters brought the morning in.

She could find nothing else to dig with in her near-empty house. Despite her desolation, she crossed the street and turned on the charm to ask the soldier for a shovel. To plant something, she told him. *Cinco minutos.* He laughed and shook his head as he handed her the spade. He offered her a swig of his tequila. She took it.

When she returned, the kitten was gone. Her bandanna lay on the other side of the yard. She ran to it. A few feet away, a dirty, bloodied grey paw lay in the dust. She scanned the yard for other parts, and found the rest of the cat, still in one tiny ragged piece, twenty feet from the neighbours' dog, who was asleep beside her back steps.

Dani carried the body over to the gravesite on the end of the shovel and wrapped it back up in the bandanna. Fighting back the urge to throw up, she dug a deeper grave, and after she placed the cat in the earth, she covered it in a layer of rocks before shovelling in the dirt. She said Namaste, for James, for whatever it was worth.

Before she returned the shovel, she slammed it into the ground beside the sleeping dog. Disgusting animal! she screamed. Get out of my sight! The dog lifted his head to stare at her, then lay back down again and closed his eyes.

**THERE WAS A BAND PLAYING** at the bar-restaurant. Friends of hers, real friends, people she had come to know and love, would be there. She decided to go, to take her mind off things.

Lang, she called, when she saw him. She waved. He didn't see her. She got up and went over to where he was standing, beside a petite blonde with a pink, peeling nose. A newcomer.

Hello, she said, waving her hand right in front of his face. Would he notice her swollen face, her reddened eyes?

It took him a few seconds to focus on her. Hey, he said.

What's the matter?

He laughed. Nothing.

Lang, what's going on?

Nothing. The woman laughed, and looped her arm around his.

I'm Dani, Dani said, and thrust her hand out.

The woman nodded. Hi. She focused on the band playing, behind Dani, and wouldn't look her in the eye. The band was playing cheesy blues covers to the tourist crowd. *Layla, you got me on my knees.*

Let's go, Lang said to the woman, and just like that, they were gone out into the night.

THE JEALOUSY BONE

Dani followed them onto the sidewalk. Wait, Dani called. Can I talk to you for a sec, Lang?

Lang didn't turn around.

Dani ran to catch up. Lang, she said, I need to talk to you. Dammit. She was fighting back more tears.

What? he said, irritated.

Is something wrong? She tried to take his hand but he put it in his pocket.

No, he said. I mean, yes. I'm tripping.

Tripping. Right. Um, I'm kind of a mess right now, too. She wiped at her face with the back of her wrist. The cat died.

Cat? What cat? He was looking at the girl with him, a stupid smile on his face. Oh, right. Bummer.

Yeah, it wanted outside, so I put it out, and—

Listen, I gotta go. He motioned to the girl.

Dani nodded. Right. I forgot.

Catch you later.

**ONCE SHE CAME HOME, SHE CONTINUED DRINKING,** this time from a bottle of Damiana liquor shaped like a voluptuous woman.

She found her return ticket: three months to go. She could change it. She looked around her house and saw nothing that she could take back to remember this place for what it really was. The few warped watercolours were only reminders of the time she had been wasting. Empty bottles and votive candles told the same story. When you went away, she knew, you had to bring back something important. She would be asked to show proof of her journey. She would be expected to have gone away and changed.

That she had gone away was all she was sure of. Until she had more *recuerdos*, souvenirs, she wasn't going home.

**THE NEXT AFTERNOON,** Dani packed her shoulder bag with mangoes, cookies, bread, and enough water for the next 24 hours. She tied her fleece around her waist and took the garbage out and shoved a towel in the inch-wide gap beneath the back door, so the geckos and cockroaches and scorpions wouldn't take over while she was gone. The black metal front door had a smaller gap, for the stream of ants that moved through the house. Once she had come out of the house and locked the door, Dani plugged the gap with toilet paper.

She would bike to the surfer's beach, La Pastora. She was not one of the motley tribe of beach dwellers, but she could pretend. She would find Lang there, with his frozen eyes and white-blond hair and post-trip hangover, and he would let her stay. If the woman from last night was there, Dani would deal with that, in whatever way she could. There might be fish, cooked on the open fire along with a few potatoes. There might be tie-dyed shirts but she would overlook them, ignore the impulse to call on James, or whatever power he believed in, to get her through another night. There would be beer, bought by one of the gringo surfers, and she would pay for what she drank, whether they asked her for money or not.

She would want to pay for everything. But what she wanted wouldn't matter. Whatever Lang wanted to do to her, she would let him.

# FEEDING ON DEMAND

**I'M LOST IN THE RHYTHM** of roadside safety posts, flashing past like half-smoked cigarettes. I want a cigarette. I can't have one. I want one. I can't have one.

"What would hawks do without telephones?" you say. You're driving us to Toronto, on Highway 7, back to Pearson Airport after our family visit, where a plane will be waiting to take us home. The scenic route, you call it. Your memory two-lane.

"What?" I say, pulled out of my nicotine reverie. I've been tuning you out since Silver Lake.

"All they do is perch on the poles. Look. Another one."

I don't look. I've suddenly become deeply engrossed in biting the baby's nails off, her soft twig fingers comical between my huge digits. The nails half-peel, half-chop away when my teeth bite down.

"Seventeen," you say. "Amazing."

I'm holding Amy in the football position, to help her get the richest milk. I'm trying everything I can to satisfy her, but she still won't stop crying until she's got a breast in her face. This

163

is normal, they say. This is to be expected, certain times of the day, growth spurts, circumstances. But there are no special circumstances for Amy, that I can see. She cries and I feed her. We haven't had a decent sleep in months.

You say, "If we get pulled over, I'm not paying the fine."

"It's a four hour trip," I say. "You want her to scream?"

You were thinking of me when you booked the tickets. Your idea to visit now, before the rush, the cheaper ticket price, the empty airports, now that we are travelling with a baby. Who can get into the spirit of Christmas in an Ontario November? It's all just mud and wind. The radio stations haven't started up the carols. The wrapping paper is still full price. You made the arrangements when I was still in hospital, eating out of plastic compartmentalized plates, glad of the separation. You read me the itinerary, flying into Ottawa, out of Toronto, renting a car to take us into the Valley. For weeks after Amy and I came home, all you could do was plan the details. I was too overwhelmed to do anything but nod.

**I CLOSE MY EYES AND TRY TO IMAGINE US** loving each other. We used to make love with candles burning, imagining ourselves in deepest India with the corresponding positions. Now the goodnight pats you give my shoulder are substitutes: a symbol of affection the way Kraft singles are symbols of cheese. You look at my breasts, my belly, my face, then smile weakly and close your eyes. I'm not really complaining. If your eyes didn't close, mine would. Becoming an exit ramp for a nine pound baby is not a move towards sensuality. But that middle trimester was a whole other thing. Remember?

I called you at work one afternoon and asked you to pick up dessert. I'd made tortilla soup, to satisfy a craving, and I wanted something sweet to end the meal. You came home with a chocolate cake. It was covered in thick waves of frosting, and I was so excited by you knowing what I wanted, exactly, that I spread out our Mexican blanket on the floor and placed the cake in the centre. Then, I took off my shirt: my nipples had become as brown as the icing. You scooped up ganache with your hands and rubbed it all over me, and we fed each other cake with our fingers and forgot about the soup entirely.

**MY THIGHS ARE HOT** from her spread-out body, from the crocheted blanket your mother gave her. If she stays asleep on my lap, then I can get a little rest. So far, so good; her limbs are like overcooked carrots. She's sleeping so heavily, as if the sleep is a wave and she is a boat and she is sailing, sailing, my bonnie lies over the ocean, as if she'll never come back, as if she's gone without even saying goodbye. I try to join her.

"Think they're red-tails," you say.

I jump. I'm so jumpy.

"Have to look it up."

You always do that, leave off the pronoun, so I never know if you're telling me to look it up or not bothering to say the "I." You give me just enough information, not a bit more. I'm not looking anything up. I've never been into birds the way you are, never pinned my attention like that onto anything, until Amy. Now I can't imagine what else could be worthy of all this focus. But you still have your little interests. You haven't given anything up.

You asked me on our second date, what are your passions, Marion? Our first date had been a movie, the kind of date where people get to know exactly three things about each other: how they laugh (because, it's usually a lighter film), how they eat (mouth closed or open, junk or just popcorn), and how they smell (if they're nervous, wear cologne, smoke, brush their teeth). Everything else is guesswork because they only talk during the trailers and commercial. That first night, you said, Capitalism at its finest, when the polar bear drank that icy bottle of Coke, and I agreed. Then felt my face go pink as I sipped my vat of cola.

Second dates are all about the details. You were wearing navy corduroys and a soft blue sweater, its Gap tag sticking out. My passions? I said. I thought you were being racy, coming onto me, so when I blushed, you blushed too, even your nose. You said, quickly, What kinds of things do you like to do? I mean, hobbies, you know... I laughed. Was I passionate about knitting? I did it to pass time productively, although it was coming back into vogue. Cooking? I did that to eat.

What about you? I asked. Well, you said. I'm into a lot of things. And then you gave me a list, a specialty magazine subject list, from tennis to French wine to Icelandic horses. Raptors, you called these birds, with a raised eyebrow. Not the basketball team. Then, I was happy for the clarification. Of course, I said, idiotically. Eagles are one of my favourite birds.

**WHEN WE ARRIVED** at your parents' house, you kissed your mother's aura, a smack in the air above her dangly earrings, along with a hug that assumed any contact meant affection. Your parents are distant relatives. It's your family's modus operandi. I shook hands all around, feeling the ring on my finger dig into my skin with every squeeze.

Everyone kept saying that Amy has my nose. Oops, got your nose. Tip of the thumb between the pointer and middle finger, a wedge of flesh that's supposed to have come right off the face like a chunk of banana, like a bud breaking off a branch. When the bough breaks. All of it's about pain and laughing, as far as I can tell. Getting through something, mockingbirds that don't sing, looking glasses that get broke, blackbirds that nip off noses, ashes ashes, we all fall down. They kept looking at her, and then at you, trying to find as much of you in her face as they could.

She has your eyes. That's something.

That whole trip was like falling over something I didn't see, then hitting the ground, hard. I didn't know, for instance, that your sister has lost three babies and won't talk to anyone who's had one. Or how much your father likes lecturing on the pitfalls of modern architecture, although I did reflect on his words from under four quilts in the

THE JEALOUSY BONE

unheated bedroom of that stone farmhouse with its strange white Ionic columns stuck onto the front. I didn't realize that people from the West are failures, softies, people who wouldn't be able to make it in "Real Canada" without a plastic bubble, whale song and the scent of rain pumped in. And, thanks to your amazing communication skills, I didn't find out until two minutes before they met us at the door that they thought we were married.

They wouldn't get it, you said, as you wrestled Amy's car seat out of the backseat. They might make us sleep in separate beds. I looked for a smile on your face, but you weren't joking. Here, you said, ducking behind the passenger door, so the people waving from the porch wouldn't see. You handed me a silver band. Slip this on.

What? I asked. Are you joking? We had talked about marriage nearly every week during the pregnancy. Both of us had agreed to wait until the baby was older, so she would know that it wasn't just because of her. Now family history was being written. Now she would forever be told that no one was invited to the wedding but her. Ha ha.

Just act natural, you said. Think of it as a practice run.

Thank you, I said, to your relatives, over and over, glaring at you every chance I had. I can't believe it either.

**AFTER A FIVE MINUTE NAP,** in which I dream we're late for the flight, I wake with a start.

"Where are we?" I ask, looking out at more grey fields and lines of leafless trees scratching an empty sky.

"Thirty two kilometres from Tweed," you say. "Actinolite's coming up. Used to be a bear there, in a cage. Used to buy Cokes for it."

I look at you for the first time in miles. You're grinning.

"It's true," you say. "A black bear."

"What?"

"He drank pop, right out of the bottle."

"You're kidding."

You shake your head.

"What happened?" I say. "Where's the bear now?"

The grin fades. You shrug like you had nothing to do with it, no emotional connection whatsoever. "Dead. That was years ago."

What about that damned Coke commercial, on our first date? Why didn't you tell me this back then? It would have been a good story. I might have laughed. It makes me realize that half the time I don't know what goes on in your head. Maybe that's a good thing. The way you look at Amy, I wonder if you give her much thought at all.

I thought we both wanted this. Thought it was pre-ordained by some magical hand just because your sperm had managed to circumvent my diaphragm. We were just starting out. I assumed that fatherhood would come in naturally, the way breast milk does.

"Bears don't like soft drinks," I say.

"I'm telling you, this one only liked Coke."

"Just like the polar bear." You don't know what I'm talking about, so you ignore my comment.

"We probably rotted his old stomach right out."

Amy stirs at your laughter and flings an arm above her head.

"I can't believe your parents let you do that. They seem like such nice people."

You pretend not to hear my tone. "We were kids," you say, loudly. "Everyone did it."

Amy's eyes are open, suddenly, as if I've dropped two black buttons onto her face.

"Hello there," I say to her blank angelic gaze, and immediately she starts to fuss. I lift my shirt, push her face-first into the boob, like a pie throw in reverse. She suckles as if it's been weeks.

"Think that's wise?"

You're looking at us. I stroke Amy's ear. She hums with every swallow. Where does all this milk come from? It's so plentiful that it runs out of her mouth and collects sweetly, then sourly, behind her ears.

"Teaching her to satisfy her sadness with food," you say. "Isn't that how bulimia starts?"

You're serious.

"You're serious."

You know what comes next. The snap in my voice, the baby crying despite the raw nipple out there, ready for her, the comments thrown between us like darts three feet away from the board. Both of us scoring nearly every time. It's obvious, and completely understandable, and very sad: having a fake marriage and chocolate swirls and a blend of my nose and your eyes is not going to be enough to sustain us.

"Stop it!" you yell, at the screaming baby, or me, I can't tell. I cover Amy's head with my hand, blood pulsing in the fontanelle like a creek under a skim of ice. The veins at your temple are standing out, a fence over the thinnest point of bone in the body. With a modest amount of pressure, anyone could push through.

**WHEN WE GET TO THE CORNER** where the bear once lived, there's an empty cage with flurries flying through the bars. You slow the car down to negotiate the turn.

"See?" you say. "There it is."

The remains stand like an old gravesite, dead weeds pushing through the cracked cement. I wonder if the bear's ghost paces its small floor space, looking for a way out, or for Coke.

"Thank you for sharing that," I say. "This is a wonderful part of the country."

"She can't still be eating," you say.

"Yes," I lie. "This bear only likes milk."

**WE DRIVE ON, WORKING GRIMLY TOWARDS TORONTO.** The overpasses we drive under are spray-painted with proclamations, pleas, the simple facts. Julia loves Rob 4 ever. The Lord is coming! Will U Marry me (George)? In a gravy brown landscape, bright blue paint becomes the only relief.

I want a cigarette. I also want Amy to be four, right now. I want her to be in a booster seat behind you, kicking the general area behind your ribs, your kidneys. I want that vibration going through you. I want to see if you'll still hold me responsible for her behaviour. For her, in general.

Make her stop, you might say. More likely, you'd say, If I feel one more kick I'm stopping to let you out. I can't be sure you wouldn't.

I want her to be fourteen and sulking behind me, the furthest point in the car she can get from you. I want it all to happen now, to have it rain down on you like a storm of nails. I want you to feel it all, immediately.

More than anything, I want this trip to be over.

The traffic thickens as we get closer to the city. We fight relentlessly, despite our exhaustion. Amy wakes, cries, eats, dozes, a reliable pattern of self-soothing that you simply cannot accept.

"They're my breasts," I tell you. "They're doing what breasts do."

You keep looking over at her suckling mouth. You're not paying attention to the merging lanes. I tell you to watch out; you don't.

In the next moment which expands to hold us like a hand, cupping smoke, I lock eyes with you. What passes between us is more than what has passed between us in months. This is not what we wanted. This has never been our intention. We had no intentions but good ones and where have they all gone? What's that song from grade school, Where have all the flowers gone, long time passing? And yet in that look I see what I've wanted: this life sinking in. We're parents, together. We have this little baby between us.

We're heading towards more white cigarette posts and the ditch they should be guiding us away from. Watch out! I scream, and I pray aloud for you to pull us back onto the road. Amy, pressed into my breast with my helpless, useless, ring-free hands, is nursing hard, again.

# FROZEN SHOULDER

**MIRIAM IS EATING A COFFEE CRISP.** With her eyes shut it tastes like it could be healthy. In between the gusts of the stop-and-start wind, she hears noises. Horses in the distance, the grind of machinery, bees. Closer, she hears the snap of twigs and a shift in the underbrush as she waits at the edge of the woods behind the hospital. She opens her eyes to the impossible geometries of a dragonfly's wings, concentrated neuroses on an overhanging branch.

Dialogue has broken down. Miriam speaks / rants / pleads / whispers / cries / talks calmly to Lily but Lily does not respond. She has become a cat. Cats do what they want. Damn the floor-to-ceiling sheers. Damn the vases and lamps they knock over like dominoes. Damn the consequences.

**A COUGAR WAS SHOT** in Sooke yesterday. They're still looking for another one in Saanich, the area where Miriam lies on her back in the grass, watching contrails and smelling wild roses whose petals should've blown off a month ago. They're warning people to keep their children and pets inside. Like it's that easy; like people will listen. She thinks of those people at garbage dumps, photographing bears, getting attacked and still more people going out.

**LILY MIGHT NOT GET BETTER.** This circulates in Miriam's brain like a mantra gone horribly wrong. If she had a partner to bounce things off, she thinks, her voice an echo that would return to her from his solid mass, they might have been able to handle this on their own.

But Daniel Unarsson was in her life only long enough to drop off his genes. As if they were in need of mending and she the seamstress. She sewed them up, from a pattern for blood and bone, into something she thought would stick around. Instead, Miriam made a Lily.

The fishing was more lucrative than a knocked-up girlfriend. Daniel returned to Iceland before he saw the white-blonde luminescence, the Atlantic eyes that sailed out of her. He left before Lily was Lily, before she could make an impression. Miriam tried calling her baby Lily Miriamsdottir, just for fun, but it didn't fit into her mouth or her life. Bye bye Daddy. *Bless bless.* Intermittent shipments of facial scrub from the Blue Lagoon and fjallagros throat lozenges do not qualify as child support.

**WHEN THE BREEZE STOPS AGAIN,** she listens. She gets up on her knees and peers into the woods; the eyes of poplar bark stare back. Miriam springs to her feet and jumps back a metre. Jesus, she thinks. My nerves are shot.

Her right arm is no good. It hangs like its own animal, holding on by its teeth to her shoulder. Miriam can't even lift a teacup with her right hand anymore, which is jeopardizing her work at the British gift shop. Her shoulder blares like a radio. You can nearly see through bone china but Miriam cannot move it. She tries to block out the pain, but even out here in the irrigated grass, the colour of New Age healing, it's too loud. There is no getting away.

Behind the applause of the poplar leaves, the birds are singing. She has heard that you should listen for this, that their silence is an inverted alarm. She lies down on her back once more, splinting the bad arm against her side. The wind starts again and she closes her eyes: it sounds simple, like the real thing, like the sea in a shell.

What kind of pain makes you stop eating? What would Lily tell her, if she decided to talk? How does she like her coffee? Has she even tasted coffee yet?

**THE GIRL ON THAT ISLAND UP NORTH** was walking the line where the forest meets the beach when a cougar leapt at her and clamped his mouth around her throat. She was an American. It wasn't a cougar to her, but a mountain lion. They call them mountain lions down there. Both of them are pumas. The girl was not really a girl, either, but a young woman, on a kayaking trip with friends from high school. A rose by any other name. Miriam wonders, if we name a thing does it have more power or less? We give things their due respect by calling them what they are. But how can we name what's coming for us if we don't know what's out there?

Her arm throbs. The wind dies down. There it is again – a rustling, a snap. She thinks, it would really be something, me out here, a cat pouncing, while my yellow-skinned daughter sits on a sofa talking about why she will eat nothing but carrots and ice.

**THERE ARE OTHER THINGS BEYOND THEM BOTH,** beyond this one. Earthquakes are the top of the threat list, and recently there have been emergency readiness classes at the community centre. Miriam was asked to be an anchor house, because her house is on a corner. She declined the request, saying she wasn't sure how long they'd be there, they were only renting, and so on. But it was denial, pure and simple, and she knew it. How can you be aware of being in denial? She didn't know.

Other threats, external, that she wants to ignore: the various uniformed men who look like safe, honest policemen to children and who are really only security guards and parking attendants. The classic white vans that patrol neighbourhoods at 3 pm, waiting for girls walking home from school. Bullies who don't like the colour of your socks. Speeding cars driven by teenagers, falling pieces of metal from airplanes. A cougar is in a different category altogether, but still, an external threat. Lily's problem is what Miriam thinks of as chosen: a wrong choice. An internal problem, not only because it's inside her body but because Lily was once inside hers, where danger had been nebulous and had unseen, mystical results.

**I WISH I COULD SAY IT WAS RARE** but it isn't, said Mr. Feldman. He is Lily's principal: he said this to Miriam when he drove Lily home from school after she fainted in class. There are people to talk to. Good people.

Good people are churchgoers and farmers to Miriam. Schoolteachers and firefighters. Toy store owners. People selling books with chicken soup in them. People who dole out soup in yellow kitchens. Mothers who make homemade soup for their daughters, and daughters who eat two goddamned bowlfuls and say thank you before racing out the door. Good people. Her kind of people. But what could they possibly do for Lily?

The girl on the island, she ended up all right, but Miriam wonders how it would feel to be her parents. To know that a cougar had held your baby; to have been that close to having your child taken, and then to have her beside you again, everything the same except for those teeth marks under gauze.

## HELLO MY NAME IS MIRIAM. MY DAUGHTER IS —

Miriam wonders if that would do it. Would her own death by cougar be the stick pulled out to make the ball go Kerplunk? My daughter used to have folds in her forearms, she thinks; knees like dinner rolls. She used to go through boxes of cereal in a day and a half. She used to hold my hand when we crossed the street and I know that's over but it was the only time I knew my power. I just want something I can hold again.

When Lily was twelve, an older boy made a comment. When are you due? he asked Lily as she played on the beach. Miriam had wanted to push him into the lake and hold him there until his cruelty washed away. Instead, she said nothing, kept looking into her *Chatelaine* like chicken quesadillas were the most exciting things. When Lily came to her that night in tears, Miriam tried to downplay the whole thing. He's just a boy, she told her. He probably has a crush on you.

Now fifteen-year-old Lily eats ice cubes from a bowl, one at a time, like olives. Now Lily eats carrots julienned into the finest pieces possible. Miriam used to like that word, the camber in her mouth as she said it. The richness of the term for cutting such a dull vegetable into delicate strips.

It started out with Lily trying a mono-diet. *Gesundheitstag*. People in Germany do it all the time, Lily said. They eat one kind of fruit for a day, to clean their systems out. Lily did this for two weeks. Her bones started appearing, her belly disappeared, her face lost its ice cream-loving roundness, her eyes were sparks. It didn't matter that she saw stars when she stood up. She was thin, and she jumped around the house like a foal, chomping on Granny Smiths.

**GESUNDHEIT**. Miriam swallows her sneezes in the field. The weak and sick ones get taken first.

Last month, on vacation, the two of them sat on that same beach under a fickle sun. Miriam wanted to walk the ridge, the top of the small mountains that lined the lake. To feel the trees like shag carpet underfoot, to be that far away from the scene on the sand below.

On the beach, Lily was smiling, looking at the blue-green water. She was folded down onto the quilt, hugging knees to ribs. The other kids had already thrown their t-shirts off and gone running into the lake; they shrieked at the cold mountain water and dove in and out of it like drunken dolphins. Lily watched. Her sweatshirt stayed on.

She refused the Delicious apple Miriam offered. Flesh of my flesh... Miriam ate it instead and Lily turned up her CD player to muffle the crunching. The apple phase had been over months before. How could she have been so insensitive?

**MIRIAM HAS BLUE EYES**, too, and vague hair, and uncertain skin. Her nose is thin and her lips are pale and her neck is long but not elegant. She smells like jasmine soap and hot cotton. Her body has the requisite curves. She closes her eyes at red lights. She is prone to tipping her head to one side when she is overcome. Wow, she says, half under her breath and it could be utter pain or amazement she is melting into: everything gets the same reaction. She has a job in a store where she must choose every movement with care and a Lily at home who will not E A T

except for – a) or b) or c)

and won't talk to her anymore.

She wonders, will the scent of this chocolate bar attract the cougar? She wonders, am I out of my mind?

**DON'T PUSH, THE FAMILY DOCTOR SAID**. Unlike during Lily's birthing, when the urge to propel that baby out of her was greater than the risk of torn flesh, Miriam hasn't. Act on her cues, he said, let

THE JEALOUSY BONE

Lily take the reins, and Miriam has become as pliant as the playdough she used to make on the stove. She remembers that recipe better than anything else she's made for Lily: her standard repertoire of "meals for two" have blurred in her mind to mush. That dough was the only reason she kept cream of tartar in the house. It's still at the back of the spice rack, box coated in dust.

**SPARTAN. PACIFIC QUEEN. ROYAL GALA. BRAEBURN.** Once she realized Lily was not backing down, Miriam loaded up her cart, hoping the variety might provide more than her favourite green apples. Miriam bought gouda and almond butter too, hoping Lily might decide to embellish.

She didn't. She moved onto grapes, because of their purifying qualities. She lost more weight. Then it was Brazil nuts. And now, the carrots that are turning her hands and feet yellow. Miriam has to hand it to her, she always picks healthy foods. But half a cup of nuts per day has never been enough to keep anyone healthy. Never enough to add even an ounce to a ninety-pound girl whose eyes have lost their blaze.

**WHILE LILY WAS STILL ATTACHED TO HER** by umbilical cord, Miriam held her to her belly and cried. This slick new being, honed to a point from the tectonic movement of skull through birth canal, this child beginning to root for a nipple, was Lily. Lilliputian. Lily of the Valley. Casablanca. These were the private names Miriam would later caress her baby's ears with while they sat on the veranda, nursing. But when the cord still pulsed and Lily suckled for the first time, when Miriam's whole body consolidated into breast, she cried into her daughter's matted hair and everyone thought it was joy. It could not have been named then, anyway. It wasn't until Miriam found herself screaming at Lily to eat something more than fruit that she was reminded of what it was: the absolutes of parenting. The loss of any remaining vestiges of control.

FROZEN SHOULDER

**MIRIAM HEARS THE LEAVES MOVING AGAIN.** They say that cougars spot you long before you can see them, so why does she bother worrying? It must be squirrels, she thinks, or varied thrushes. Everything is just out of her sight. It doesn't matter. She's not leaving this spot where the poplars are clapping for her every move. She hasn't had this much attention in years.

**MIRIAM IS FOURTEEN** again. She's having a Halloween sleepover while her parents are at a party. After the trick or treating, the girls sit around in the dark and tell stories about death while they gorge on kisses and chocolate bars. She has never felt as popular, never as satisfied with her life. Then, at one in the morning, a knock at the window sends them all to hide under the kitchen table. She doesn't know what to do. Miriam can only chant, "Phone my grandmother! Phone my grandmother!" and huddle under the formica. All the girls hide but Jean, who lives on a farm five miles from town. Jean walks up to the front door and opens it, as if she's been expecting someone. Miriam and the others hide their faces in their laps. But no one is there, except the jack-o-lantern, already caving in on itself in the rain.

**ADHESIVE CAPSULITIS.** Miriam counts the rolling syllables as she repeats her affliction to herself. Two months ago, she heard the pop of tendon as she lifted a bag of potatoes from the trunk, and now she can't lift a glass. There are good people inside for her too. But Miriam doesn't go in. She stays rooted to the grass, listening for the birds to stop singing.

**HELLO MY NAME IS MIRIAM.** Before she started passing out, my daughter used to bag groceries at a health food store and she learned too much on her breaks. She calls it fasting / purifying / cleansing / proper living but she's starving herself and I don't know how to stop it.

The girl survived the cougar. Maybe this brush with death will protect her as she moves through her days. Those teeth marks a talisman around her neck.

**MIRIAM'S COFFEE CRISP IS FINISHED;** she sits with her back to the woods and cradles her useless arm, while thin, electric-blue damselflies land on her legs in ones and twos. She remembers how they used to alight on Lily's hair when she was swimming, like temporary barrettes, and how she was afraid of them, thinking they were dragonflies. No dragons in there, Miriam told her. Nothing but damsels looking for a place to rest.

# BORING BABY

**IT'S KIND OF FREAKING ME OUT,** to be honest. You're offering me the one thing I've wanted more than anything—until this morning, I hadn't had a sip in, like, six months.

A baby. Not a cleanse. I had a baby. God, that tastes amazing. What is it, Guatemalan?

I thought so. I know my beans.

Yeah, she's sweet. She's a baby.

Oh, what the hell. I'll be honest with you. I wish I could give that baby some coffee directly. Because here is something I know for sure: I have a boring baby.

I tell her this. I say, you're boring, when she just lies there, watching the dust move. I say let's get this show on the road. I look at the other parents carting around their blobs in pastel velour onesies. They look happy, placid, as if this is the pinnacle of human existence, cooing at the baby bunnies in the petting zoo, watching the lambs harass the mother sheep for milk. The baby humans sit there, some of them laughing and pointing at the fuzzy ducklings. If they're like my baby, they sleep through most of it. Wake up, I say. Stop being so dull. Do you think I'm here for my own good?

Don't look at me that way. I'm serious. This kid is as active as an end table.

Mind if I have another cup?

**IF YOU REALLY WANT TO KNOW,** the baby looks like Tim. She has squints for eyes and straight, poky hair. Her head is half of her. Her hats nearly fit me.

No, I'm not a *pinhead*. Look at me. I'm just petite-headed.

But anyway. This morning started out like every other these days. I woke while it was still dark, with dead arms and that baby freaking out in her crib. By the time I got the feeling back she was on full blast, and when she latched on it was with a vengeance, little hiccup sobs still making her body twitch.

Tim moaned, turned over, put his second pillow over his head and fell back into sleep. Once the baby finally had her fill of me, she passed out. I moved her into the middle of our king-size and tried to go to sleep, pillow over my own head.

I dreamt she was half the size of a cell phone. I stuck her in my pocket and went to an Arcade Fire show. After the concert, she was still sleeping and I thought, good, see, no harm done. I took her out and threw her into the air and caught her as she fell back to me. I did it over and over, trying to make her laugh, but she started screaming, she was really working it up—until Tim jiggled my shoulder. Toni, he mumbled. For once, he'd heard her first.

**BY 5:00 A.M. I WAS ON THE ROAD.** Every light was green for me. I floated through the empty streets like a jubilant skater girl, nothing to slow me down. The boulevards were getting sprinkled despite severe water restrictions and the sound of the water under my wheels made me think of eighteen-wheelers on real highways, rushing past in a sudden summer squall, the car being pushed and pulled by torrents of speeding air and spray. All those signs overhead, so many possible exits. Another downside to being on Vancouver Island, although most people, unlike me, come and never want to leave: no triple digit limit.

When I reached my "highway," 80 felt like 120 and I joined the light traffic heading north. There were people in the cars around me, people who needed coffee and didn't want 7-ELEVEN. People who couldn't wait to get off this island. People not even awake but starting their long journey across the country or across the globe. People who liked to drive as the light comes in. People driving their children to the ferry to go back to the other parent after a weekend of gaming and pancakes for dinner. People driving a screaming infant around in hope that the speed and rush and noise of a car on a road would be enough to make it shut up before they started to break down, open, apart.

It was so quiet in my car. The car seat base could have been something else entirely strapped onto the seat.

I don't *know* what. Nothing comes to mind right now. But still.

**I DROVE. THE ROAD ROSE SLIGHTLY** and to my right a valley was fleecy with fog. Beyond this there was ocean and then land, a breast of an American mountain peak pushing into an orange sky's mouth.

Oh, my God, listen to me. It was a beautiful snow-capped mountain. It had nothing at all to do with suckling.

I let myself take dangerously long glances, then descended to field level again and smelled the cornstalks growing their white-tasselled heads off, level with the road. Something Tim would find beautiful.

Something he would stop for, to shoot film of, to make us late for whatever we were heading for.

But Tim can't drive. He can't swim either. He rides a bike but only when absolutely necessary. Tim is also afraid to go on planes, hasn't set foot in an airport since well before you-know-when. He is not alone in this, I know. But, in him, it seems like a weakness. He just has too many of these "quirks," as he calls them. I'm not as brave as you, he tells me. You should have seen his face when I was in labour. My. God. I think he would've fainted if he wasn't afraid of hitting his precious head.

I used to work as a pharmaceutical rep. I used to drive these roads, and other roads, back east in Wrong-tario, plying my wares to sleep-deprived doctors and disinterested pharmacists, pushing pills to save lives. I used to dress up for my job, jackets and skirts and pumps and lacy underwear. I liked my job. I miss my job.

Now I live in faded yoga garb, the uniform in my new place of employment. This esteemed job involves sitting in a house for 23 hours a day and calling it a life.

They call it Baby Jail for a reason.

Yeah, that's what I said. Baby Jail.

**I KEPT DRIVING, PAST FIELDS AND BILLBOARDS** and those rusting tractors that people pay $8 to see. Then it came up on my left: the turnoff for the airport. Does the sign make you laugh, too? International. This backwater little city that poses as a hot spot is nothing more than a tourist shoppe (Ye Olde English for the suckers who believe it) and a warehouse for old folks. You can't even find a decent dessert here past 9 pm, never mind a classy nightclub. But that sign gets me thinking, I'll tell you. Places beyond the manicured hedge.

What do you think I did?

You're right. I did.

**TIM WOULD HAVE BEEN HAVING FITS** if he'd been there, watching the scene. Mainly the security line-up. We're talking a hundred bleary-eyed passengers sucking back mega-hits of Starbucks. They looked like smokers furiously puffing on the church stairs before a wedding.

Didn't you hear that transporting all liquids on planes was banned, as of the weekend, when that plot was foiled? They say it involved a family: a man, his wife, their young baby. I know. It's sick. Explosives in the bottle packed into the diaper bag. No one said whether it was breast milk or Nestlé.

I was really ticked off that I hadn't pumped. If I had, I could've joined those sad people in a toast to the light. What light... in yonder window breaks. I've always loved that line. But I'd like to know what harm one short medium roast can do, anyway.

Tim doesn't know Shakespeare or shit about shit and yet he's the new expert. Reads all the books about children, watches all the shows, surfs all the message boards. He's afraid of SIDS, SARS, HIV, ADD, and many other alphabetical conglomerates. I tell him to stop reading so much, that he's going to get MSP, Munchausen Syndrome by Proxy, and cause the baby to be sick. He doesn't find this funny.

At least his pathological fears do not include diapers. Or jerking off. I'm getting damned good at faking sleep while the bed gently rocks.

Oh, I wanted a coffee bad. I wanted to stand in line with these people, wanted to go through the gate and the next gate and so on until I was on one of those vinyl seats that sigh when you sit down to wait. But Tim and his online mothers group say that caffeine crosses into the milk.

What's the problem, I asked him, the day after the birth, when I was so tired I wanted a gallon of espresso.

It's caffeine, he said, underlining it with his voice. That can't be good for an infant.

Do you know when a baby stops being an infant? Me neither. But I think I've got a lot of time ahead of me. Anyway, I asked Tim, What does it do to a kid?

He didn't say anything, because he hadn't Googled it yet. But he took the baby from my lap, where she was sucking on her fist, as if already they both didn't trust me with my desires.

**AT THE LAKE LAST WEEK,** I took her out of her strollered cocoon and stuck her bare toes in the water. There were divers in the lake searching the silt for a certain kind of newt, one that scientists were studying for clues on regeneration. A guy waiting for the divers told me: they cut off their limbs and watch them grow back. The cells go back to how they were before birth, he said. Then they start growing again. One day, he said, shrugging his shoulders. One day maybe humans will do the same.

When Tim found out how deep it was where they were diving, he was shocked that no one had put up a sign.

It's dangerous, he said.

It's only dangerous if you can't swim, I said.

Uh, well... he said.

Oh, right.

The baby was contracting her abs to get herself out of the water, fussing her little face off.

What about kids? he said. That isn't safe.

Tim, I said. They don't just get up and dive right in. Look at her. She hates it.

She's still half asleep, he said. And that water is damned cold.

Honestly, I wanted to throw the baby in. I wanted to show him the natural instinct to swim. But instead I just handed her over to him and stripped down to my underwear, his boxer shorts, my big boobs in their stretched cotton holster. What are you doing? he asked, stupidly. Toni, what the hell are you doing?

I walked right in without looking back. It was warmer than it is today.

Tim calls it PPD. Denial. Cold heart. He studies every tiny thing I do, as if they're clues to a mystery. There is no mystery. I gave birth to a baby who is as dull as her father, who isn't interested in the world, whose whole universe is milk.

Can I help it if I wanted to deliver someone else? Someone to replace the monotony of Tim? I didn't want to replicate him, dammit. This baby is already a disappointment. Already, she's letting me down.

No, I'm not going to a support group. Not unless they serve real coffee.

**AT THE AIRPORT, THERE WAS A WOMAN IN LINE** ahead of me. She was carrying a toy stuffed rabbit. She asked the bunny what it wanted, and then answered for it.

Grande vanilla latté, she said, in a wee bunny voice, then turned to me and used the baby talk: we're going to have a long day.

I looked more closely at her, and her bunny. They were dressed in the same outfits. I mean really, the identical flipping clothes, everything from the shoes to the wire frame glasses.

Where are you going? I asked this loonie, hoping I never had to sit on a plane with her, ever.

Phoenix, she answered. I guess I was staring at the toy because she said, this is my wittle baby. A mini-me, she said, then giggled like a four-year-old.

Your baby, I said.

Oh yes, she said. She goes everywhere with me. We have ten matching outfits and I named her after my mother. Didn't mommy name you Candice after her mommy? At this she jiggled the bunny on her hip, like I've seen mothers do. If I did that to my baby, her head would fall off her neck like a scoop of spumoni.

And where are you going? she asked me.

Montreal, I said, before I even formulated the thought, as if this word had been sitting in my mouth, ready to jump.

What's in Montreal? she asked.

I smiled and pointed to the counter. Latté time.

**TIM USED TO SING TO ME** when I was pregnant. "Baby Beluga" was his favourite, and he thought he was being cute. He loved to rub my white belly with coconut oil and talk to the foetus, explaining the room we were sitting in, telling stories. When he wasn't around, I told the baby things about us, about him, things I thought she should know.

No, you don't really need to know.

One night when I was so bored and tired of being stuck on the floor with my ass in the air, on my hands and knees, trying to get the baby to flip into "optimal foetal position," I told Tim I was taking him out to the movies. We ended up at the IMAX, watching the oldest IMAX film out there, *Whales*. I thought the water and mammals would help turn this kid around, the way my cousin went into labour after watching *The Blair Witch Project*. The baby kicked all through the movie, but didn't turn. I, however, blubbered through most of it, watching dolphins race and click and squeal. Watching the baby humpback with its mother about to make the perilous journey from

Hawaii to Alaska, I was afraid, just like Patrick Stewart, the narrator, wanted me to be.

Hormones really do fuck a person up.

**IT MUST HAVE BEEN HORMONES TALKING** when I met Tim. He duped me. He wore t-shirts that said FCUK, and Same Same, but Different. He drank beer from Belgium and used aromatherapy hair products. His father had a business of importing vehicles with the steering wheel on the other side, and he was making mad amounts of money at this. Did my parents even know that the money in Europe had changed to Euros?

Tim himself was making decent cash as a food photographer, another misleading fact. I thought that a man who brought out food's best on film would also love food, and thus, love me. But his idea of a decent meal is street meat followed by Baskin-Robbins. He loves to eat KD right out of the pot.

Ah, shit. You don't really need to know this, either, all right? I already know it, and telling you again is making me yawn. I don't have to tell you any more about Tim's little habits. He's just as dull as a spoon.

That his hair sticks up like that British actor in *Room with a View* makes no difference either. Me and my old hormones apparently thought it would.

**WHAT'S IN MONTREAL? I DON'T KNOW ANYMORE.** I know *I'm* not there, not even on my once-a-month visit to the English-friendly pharmacies. I miss the place. I miss the French, the way the words made my tongue and lips move, the way I was starting to get jokes without any translation.

Okay, I miss flirting with Gilles, too, one of the pharmacists who took me out for lunch on the last day I visited his business.

The west, he said, lighting up a cigarette, is full of people who hate the east. But the east is not full of west-haters. Do you want to be around that much bitterness?

But won't the bitterness turn to happiness, when they're finally free of here? I asked.

It may be, he said, taking a drag and letting the smoke out from one side of his lovely mouth. Do you hate it here?

No, I said, looking into my coleslaw. I'm not leaving for hate.

Ah, he said. L'amour. We should have had this lunch a long time ago, non?

**IT WAS WHILE I WAS IN LINE FOR A TICKET** that I started leaking. Someone's little monster started crying and I was lactating like a crying mother of God statue. I looked down at my purse and realized all I had in there was a couple of diapers and an extra sleeper, plus the cell phone and my wallet. What could I possibly have been thinking? Montreal. If I showed up like that, or in a gift shop sweatshirt, they'd have me arrested. I couldn't go to Montreal. Thunder Bay, then? Edmonton?

It was almost my turn when I saw my supervisor in the e-ticket kiosk. At least, I could see his boots and his hat. He couldn't see me, not yet, and hadn't seen me since my mat leave began, but in about thirty seconds he was going to come around the console and recognize me and ask me where I was going.

And what would I say? Oh hi, yes, the baby, she's lovely. At home with Daddy while I go for a wee holiday in my wet t-shirt, no luggage, no destination in mind really, just gotta get away, haha.

Excuse me, I said to the man behind me with the newspaper, but could I have that flyer?

He gave me the Dell insert and with the paper in front of my face, I was out of there in a flash.

I was in short term parking. But I only got one ticket.

**SO WHERE DID I GO?** You'd think there would be homing devices in my breasts, leading me back to the lair. That if I'd gotten on a plane to Quebec, I would've forced the thing down in the plaza parking lot near our house because a baby needed her fix and, dammit, there was only one place to get it. But I'm not sure I came with this feature.

I *do* think La Leche League would have kicked me out by now. If it wasn't supposed to be better for everyone involved, I think I might have stopped after the first few days. I'm counting on it slimming me down now. I'm aching to get back into my pencil skirts.

Yeah, I know people who haven't lost their baby fat, too. But that's not going to be me.

**I GOT THE IDEA AS I WAS DRIVING** back into town, breasts aching. I needed to get knocked up again, quickly. Two kids so close together they're in the same class, like twins, who can entertain each other. That's it. Never mind that I'm not bleeding yet. I conceived this one when I *was* bleeding, and when I told my doctor, she said, some of us are like rabbits. We can ovulate on demand. If Britney Spears can do it, then so can I.

Eggs, I said, I demand of you, come on down.

When I pulled up beside a BMW at the stop light, I looked at the driver. He was singing along to the radio despite the early hour.

I could smell this man's leather upholstery and cologne from my car. We looked at each other. We smiled. He glanced at my chest, and kept on smiling. Thank God I'd changed into that extra shirt I had stashed in the back seat.

Eggs, are you listening? I thought. There's a man in the next car and I'm not afraid to use him.

*Of course* I was joking.

**BY THIS TIME I WAS PRETTY SURE** that the baby was probably freaking out. I imagined Tim, on the phone, getting his park mommies all strapping their progeny into their SUVs to take to the highways in search of his wife. I'm scared she'll do something foolish, he's said to them. I'm just so, so scared.

I took the fastest way home. My damned breasts were leaking again. When I got there, she was lying there, wracked with hunger and—

I slowed down in front of the house. The lights weren't on in the kitchen yet. The newspaper was still on the porch. The outside light was still pouring useless rays into the morning, something Tim turns off immediately upon waking.

They were still sleeping. I had left them, and they were having the most peaceful sleep of their lives. I left, and they didn't even notice.

I could have been right beside them, smelling their morning breath, watching them twitch in their early morning dreams. But I wasn't.

I kept on driving.

**THERE WAS NO ONE AT THE BEACH** when I got here. Of course there wasn't. It was 7 am on a weekday. The sun won't get down to the sand until at least lunchtime, and even then it won't be enough to take the chill off.

I didn't care. I was down to my underwear again in only a few seconds. This time, I took everything off and was in the water before it could register as cold.

Right. You know all this. Thanks for the towel—and this perfect brew.

God, my boobs are killing me. How long have we been here yakking? The families are starting to come in for takeover. Look at all those kids. Do you think that any of those women are happy? I mean, would you like wiping snotty noses and bums all day?

You're going swimming? That water is beautiful. There are interesting things in there, too. Like those newts. You gotta love an animal that rebuilds itself when it's broken.

I would love to join you. But what am I going to do—wait a second. Yes! It's brilliant. I just came up with a plan. Actually, before you go, maybe you could help me.

You see that family over there? The ones with the toddler in water wings? I want you to distract them for a few minutes. There's a baby in the stroller beside them. Keep them busy while I—while I relieve myself.

No, I don't mean in the bathroom. I mean these big mamas.

It's not creepy. Milk, is milk, is milk.

Can you hear that screaming? Perfect. Let's pretend we're a lesbian couple who really wants a baby. I'll take the kid for a wee walk while you ask them questions, and when I come back, the baby and I will both be satisfied.

I *know* I drank a lot of coffee. But didn't I tell you what Tim discovered? It makes a baby sleepy. Caffeine actually puts kids to sleep. That's why I can't drink it at home: if my baby were any sleepier, she'd be hibernating. This mother won't mind if her wailing banshee goes to sleep.

You won't help me. Why won't anyone help me? The lady I met here yesterday wouldn't help me, either. She told me to answer my cell phone. She told me to go home.

As if I wouldn't have.

As if I'd leave my family, just like that.

# ACKNOWLEDGMENTS

**I AM GRATEFUL FOR** everyone in my life who has supported my writing affliction, beginning with my parents and family. Many thanks to Ryan Rock, my husband and ultimate cheering section, to my dear friend and writing champion Sarah Selecky, and to Avery, my daughter. Thanks, too, to my writing compatriots: Patricia Young, Laurie Elmquist, Kari Jones, Barbara Henderson, Jill Margo, Alisa Gordaneer, Ilana Stanger-Ross, and Lisa Baldissera, as well as Gail Anderson-Dargatz, Michael Winter, John Gould, Marc Christensen, Mark Jarman, Traci Skuce and everyone else who has helped along the way.

**I AM THANKFUL FOR** the mentorship of Elisabeth Harvor through the Humber School for Writers, and for Annabel Lyon's keen eye and mentorship support through the Banff Centre's wonderful Wired Writing Studio, the Victoria School of Writing and the dearly departed BC Festival of the Arts.

THESE STORIES HAVE APPEARED in magazines: "Backstory" in *The Antigonish Review*, "Boring Baby" in *The Dalhousie Review*, "Radio Who" and "Feeding on Demand" in *The Fiddlehead*, "Frozen Shoulder" in *Wordworks*, "Jealousy Bone" in *Boulevard*, and "Appropriate" in *existere*. As well, "Chicory," "Boring Baby," and "Radio Who" were published in the Oberon anthology *Coming Attractions '07*. I am grateful to all of the editors.

# ABOUT THE AUTHOR

PHOTO | RYAN ROCK

**JULIE PAUL** was born and raised in the Ottawa Valley village of Lanark, Ontario. She now lives with her husband and daughter in Victoria, BC, where she is a writer, massage therapist, mother and teacher. Her stories, poems and essays have been accepted for publication in numerous journals, including *The Antigonish Review, The Fiddlehead, Geist, existere, Boulevard, Canadian Living* and in the anthologies *Women Behaving Badly* and *Coming Attractions '07.*